Fall to Pieces

BY VAHINI NAIDOO

AMAZON CHILDREN'S PUBLISHING

Fall to Pieces

The characters and events portrayed in this book are fictitious. Any similarity to real persons, living or dead, is coincidental and not intended by the author.

Text copyright © 2012 by Vahini Naidoo

Amazon Publishing
Attn: Amazon Children's Publishing
P.O. Box 400818
Las Vegas, NV 89149
www.amazon.com/amazonchildrenspublishing

Library of Congress Cataloging-in-Publication Data
Naidoo, Vahini.
Fall to pieces / by Vahini Naidoo. — 1st ed.
p. cm.
Summary: Knowing that two friends are lying and keeping secrets about the night another friend killed herself, seventeen-year-old Ella searches for the truth.
ISBN 978-0-7614-6217-0 (hardcover) — ISBN 978-0-7614-6219-4 (ebook)
[1. Grief—Fiction. 2. Suicide—Fiction. 3. Secrets—Fiction. 4. Friendship—Fiction. 5. Youths' writings.] I. Title.
PZ7.N1387Fal 2012
[Fic]—dc23
2011048166

Book design by Alex Ferrari
Editor: Marilyn Brigham

Printed in the United States of America (R)
First edition

10 9 8 7 6 5 4 3 2 1

To Suri,
for teaching me to love stories

Chapter One

PETAL'S GOT HER ARM UP A VENDING MACHINE. EYES FIXED on this one can of soda. She strains to reach it, but her fingers just keep scrabbling at thin air. "Shit," she says. She punches her arm around, moving the whole machine. "Get out," she singsongs at the soda. "Get out, get out, get out already."

Mark tries to catch my gaze, but I'm determined not to look at him. We're leaning against this blue railing, rusty metal flaking away between our fingers. Watching Petal. Watching, watching, watching.

I can't take it anymore. I turn toward the football field that runs away behind us, where silver rain kicks the grass. I'm seized by the sudden urge to make my skin slippery, to get closer to the wet earth.

I step out from behind the railing.

Mud licks my sneakers, and water licks my skin, curls its tongue over the yellow pages of the newspaper I'm holding. *The Sherwood High Gazette*. Like Petal, the *Gazette* is something I don't want to think about, so I fold it over the blue railing. Step farther onto the field.

Pause.

Turn, turn, turn.

Rivers of water rush over my skin, get lost beneath my clothes. The water is cold and clean, pure like the sky that it's fallen from; but it does nothing to absolve me.

I'm dirty and guilty as usual. Freezing my ass off, too.

I run my hands up and down my arms, watching the field. Watching, watching, watching. As the sprayed white lines, the boundaries from last week's game, wash away. As this guy with fire-engine red hair stands in the middle of the field, arms out. Head tilted up, up, up to the sky.

He's open, I think. Opened up to secrets whispered by the rain. Or to a lightning bolt in the chest. He stays like that for a second. Then, as if his body is weightless, ungoverned by the laws of gravity, he flops backward.

Mud explodes around him.

"Well," I mutter, "at least there's one person who's crazier than Pet."

Behind me, Mark snorts. "If there is," he says, "it's not that guy. It's you."

"Fuck you." I spin and stare him down. "I'm sane. Totally sane."

After it happened, it wasn't me with glassy eyes, lips

that barely moved. It wasn't me who whispered those words: *"What if we could find out what it was like?"*

I didn't invent Pick Me Ups.

That little bit of crazy was all Mark.

He doesn't say anything. His lip's curled ever so slightly, though. His eyes are narrowed.

God. We're supposed to be best friends. It's not meant to be like this.

Pet's still attacking the damn vending machine. Shiny brow, polished like a coin. Sweating, she's sweating. The most beautiful girl I know trying to steal from a vending machine.

It's not meant to be like this.

It wasn't, before.

"Get out," Petal whispers to the can of soda again. She smashes her face against the machine. Sprays of black Coke erupt inside it behind her face.

"Okay," Mark says. "I have to ask—what the *hell* are you doing, Pet?"

Breaking cans of soda. Wishing they were bottles of beer, probably. Glass smashes so much more dramatically.

Mark's almost laughing. There's amusement in his voice, on his face. He doesn't see the need to cry over this like I do. But then Mark hardly ever sees the need to cry.

Before, his world was an infinite number of laughs.

"Imitating Robin Hood," Petal says, her voice muffled by the machine.

Clack-clack-clack. The cans rattle against one another. Pet strings swear words together, sings them beneath her breath.

And god, I just want her to stop. I want her to stop, because whenever she does this it's a reminder of what happened. A reminder made of sticks and stones, of razor blades and penknives.

"Come on," I say, walking out of the rain, back behind the railing. "You are far from poor, *Robin*. The comparison doesn't make sense."

"So what. The accuracy of the comparison doesn't matter. Nothing matters."

Nothing matters.

I close my eyes. Against the *splish-splash-splish* of rain. Against the cold threatening to worm its way into my bones. Against those words.

I've heard them before. So many times before. On someone else's lips. Amy's.

I open my eyes. Remember why I texted them to get their asses out of class in the first place.

The newspaper.

I stalk over to the railing, snatch the paper up, and throw it to the ground next to Petal. That gets her attention. She stops attacking the vending machine and glances over at the paper sitting by her feet, its yellow paper soggy.

"Have you seen this? Have you guys *seen* this?" I ask.

"Chill, Ella," Mark says. "It's just the school newspaper." He pulls his sunglasses out of their resting place in his bird's nest of brown curls—only Mark would wear sunglasses on a day this rainy—and toys with them, unconcerned.

After all, the *Gazette* has never run anything more interesting than an article about how gross the cafeteria food is. It never has before, anyway.

"There's an article," I say. A lump crashes around in my throat. I swallow, swallow, swallow until it's gone. "It's about her. Amy."

"What?" Mark snatches up the newspaper.

Petal stops splitting her attention between the newspaper and that can of soda she's so in love with and looks up at me.

"Camille Weston wrote this," Mark says, turning the name over on his tongue. "Who is *Camille Weston*?"

"No fucking idea," I say.

"Jesus." And then he scans the meat of the article and starts laughing. Hard. Fast. Harder. Faster.

He's reading the article in Camille's voice, a breathy falsetto. "'Amy Johnson was a beautiful soul. She was the most sensitive girl I know, the quietest, and the cleverest. She always had soft, kind words for everybody.'"

Wind whips Petal's black hair around her face, Poca-hontas-style. "I'm not sure whether I should puke or go find Camille Weston and rip her guts out."

"It's such bullshit," I say. Clenched jaw. Clenched fists. Clenched gut. I try to ease everything up, relax. I'm supposed to be the sane one. "They're trying to make her sound like some nice little girl."

"I know," Mark says. God, even he's serious. He rubs a hand over his forehead, pushes up the stupid blue scarf he's got tied around his head ninja-style.

Amy loved those scarves. The scarves and the dimples, she told me once when I asked her. That's why she fell for Mark.

"I need a Pick Me Up," Mark says. "You in?"

And this is why he's the crazy one.

No. No, no, no. No way.

That's what I should say. I should stop this, stop doing this to myself. Because it's wrong. Insane. Incredibly fucked up.

Besides, I don't have time to wreck myself today, much as I usually hate Mondays. Not this Monday. Not when I'm beginning my mother-mandated volunteer work at the local child care center. Can't show up with bruises floating over my skin like landmasses across the ocean.

I shouldn't do this.

But I'm nodding my head. "Yeah. I'm in."

Mark looks at Petal. She laughs. Icy wind rips through the sound, steals all of its melody. "Do you even need to ask?"

And then she pirouettes down the path.

Actually *pirouettes*.

"Maybe she is crazier than him, after all," Mark says, hooking a thumb over his shoulder at the guy who's still lying on the field. Mud and sky all around him.

Mark heads off the way Petal went. "Coming?" he calls to me.

I stay for a second. The guy's making snow angels in the mud, as if he wants nothing more than to feel it on his skin.

Then I sigh and follow Mark because my body needs a Pick Me Up, no matter what my brain's saying. I realize halfway to the parking lot that I'm still holding the *Gazette*.

I want to throw it away. It's such trash. But I can't bring myself to do it because there was one line in the article. One line that will rumble around in my brain for the next few days.

Amy Johnson was a beautiful soul.

Chapter Two

WHEN YOUR BEST FRIEND DIES, YOU'RE SUPPOSED TO GO into mourning.

You're supposed to wear more black than usual. Smile wafer-thin smiles when people offer condolences. Stop going to school. Play your way through Radiohead's *Pablo Honey* again-again-again, because it was *her* favorite album. Tear your hair out. Cry so hard that it feels more like a desperate prayer than sadness.

I do it, all of it; I do.

But.

You're not supposed to have no idea what the fuck happened the night of your best friend's death. Not supposed to have downed a ton of alcohol, or maybe something worse, so that you remember nothing. Not supposed to hate yourself for throwing the party in the first place.

You're not supposed to blame your best friend, your shitty best friend, for leaving you all alone.

But I did. I did forget everything that happened that night. And I do blame Amy and myself. Amy for jumping. Me for not being there to catch her. For not knowing *why*.

Why.

More than anything, I want answers. Need them. The need drives me here, to the barn. Drives me up the barn stairs. I climb them with pure abandon. Reckless. As if they're a stairway to heaven.

"The first Pick Me Up is mine!" I yell to Mark and Petal.

They just look at me, still standing among the bales of hay on the bottom floor.

"Sure, whatever," Petal says.

Here, I'm the crazy one. Here, in this supposedly historical barn that the people of Sherwood insist on keeping because it's got "heritage value," I'm the crazy one. No one else ever comes to the barn. Just us. The ground floor's all creaky planks, hay, bird shit. But teenage Martha Stewarts that we are, we've attempted to spruce up the place.

There's the dartboard that Amy stole from the principal's office in the ninth grade to my left. Her old vinyls hang on the walls: Led Zeppelin, Hendrix, Queen, Radiohead. The wind plays deejay with them, and they spin, shrieking against the walls. Her scarves, gauzy and colorful, flutter from the railings on the third floor.

The third floor.

None of us has done a Pick Me Up from there. Yet.

Maybe today.

I look up, feet itching to climb those stairs.

Mark must see me looking because he calls, "Ella, it's too dangerous. If you go up there, I'll smash the gnome into a million pieces."

I stay on the second floor. Poke my head over the edge. "You wouldn't."

"Oh," he says, "but I would."

I take a deep breath, look at the stairs. Tempting. So tempting. But I shake my head, shake the thought away. It's not worth it. I can't risk losing the gnome.

Because the gnome is the only one who saw Amy die.

She didn't tell me her famous last words—and knowing Amy, they would have become an urban legend. She didn't let me see her spiral to the ground. Didn't give me a chance to stop her.

But she landed in a patch of weeds in front of my fucking garden gnome.

I'm ridiculously jealous of it.

But I'm also ridiculously attached to it. So attached that I had to hide it. The thought of my dad getting the mail every morning and sliding his eyes over its rosy cheeks and Santa hat made me feel sick. Not that Dad's even around anymore.

"Have you guys set up the gnome already?"

I tap my foot on the edge of a plank, waiting. There's a safety rail here, but it's so low that I could easily trip and fall over the edge. It's a nice feeling. Knowing that I'm so high up yet so close to the ground.

"Ella, seriously? Please let's stop with this gnome thing—" There's a note of panic in Mark's voice now. He's remembering, I can tell. He's remembering the first time we played Pick Me Ups.

I insisted on the gnome being there. On the gnome watching.

"The gnome's the only one who saw Amy," I told him. "We need a referee or something."

I sounded dumb. I am dumb. An inanimate referee?

But still.

"The gnome refs," I whisper. "The gnome refs," I call to Mark.

Petal pouts but pulls the gnome from her bag and places it on a bale of hay. "Happy?" she says.

They're always like this about the gnome. They think my need to have the gnome watch is psychotic. But I keep hoping that maybe one day the gnome will show me. Show me Amy before she fell: what her face looked like, whether she was wearing the smell of alcohol like cologne, whether she screamed.

And maybe that *is* psychotic. I don't really give a fuck. Because this gnome plan is working. Because every time I've jumped, tossed myself over the safety railing and screamed all the way down into the bales of hay, I've gotten back a piece of memory.

A tiny snippet of something that happened that night. Amy and I, fingers twisted through each other's, golden beer slopping over our wrists. Cigarettes, bright orange flares lighting up dark rooms.

Answers.

I don't know why Mark and Petal are so into Pick Me Ups, why they're oh so desperate to weave their skins into a tapestry of bruises. But I do it because I have so many questions. Because I want all the answers.

Up. I'm climbing again. Onto the safety railing.

The rickety wood creaks beneath me, threatening to break.

I can see the bales of hay below. And Mark's and Petal's faces, suffused with blood, eyes glowing. This is exciting. The fall is always exciting.

It's also fucking terrifying.

I look down. Nerves prickle up my arms, down my legs. All over my body.

"Go, Ella," Petal calls. "Go, go, go!"

If I don't do this now, I'll chicken out. My body will overpower my brain, the need in my gut. The need to fall, to hit the ground. I'll hop off the railing, walk away. Back down the stairs. To safety. To a world with no answers.

It's the question marks that do it, the ones that circle above my head, the ones that haunt me. They nudge me off the edge.

And I'm falling, falling, falling. A scream rips its way out of my throat but gets lost in a rush of air. I wait for a snippet of memory to surface. I close my eyes, expecting one to play like a reel of film in my brain. It doesn't come.

I smash into the hay on my hands and knees. The impact shatters me. I'm certain there are bits and pieces of me scattered everywhere. I feel my way through my body—*HeadNeckTorsoArmsPalmsHipsThighsCalvesFeetToes*—and bring myself back together again.

Pain is everywhere, and it steals the breath from my lungs. But I'm still whole.

I'm still whole.

Laughter spins from my mouth. Because I did this. I did this, and I didn't break.

"Okay, Ella?" Mark offers me a hand, and I take it, let him pull me to my feet. Splinters of pain still burn throughout my body. The second I'm upright, all I want is to fall again. To collapse.

Petal's grinning at me. "Now how does that make you feel?" she says, imitating the voice of our school counselor, Mrs. Andrews-but-call-me-Gladys.

I look down at my hands. The skin's split apart in a

hundred different places, tiny cuts tangling together across my palms. I look down at my calves. The skin's ripped like a laddered stocking.

Wrecked. I'm wrecked.

But there's blood pounding in my ears. Air skyrockets through my lungs.

"Awesome," I tell Petal. "Awesome."

Pick Me Ups make the world go from a grainy seventies picture to a high-definition image in ten seconds flat. They bring you back from the fucking dead.

Worth it, despite the pain.

So far I've broken: finger. I've sprained: ankle. I have bruises: everywhere.

And how does that make me feel? Amazing. Amazing. Amazing.

"So," Mark says. He grabs the gnome off the bale of hay Pet stood it up on, hands it to me. "What's our ref say?"

Ceramic, cool glazed clay between my fingers. I don't want to do this. Don't want to meet the gnome's eyes. The world's already getting grainier, the high-definition picture fading along with my high. Because I know I've fucked up; I know that I didn't get a memory, didn't see Amy.

Still, I do it. I meet the gnome's beetle-black eyes and read my verdict. Failure.

It's as if I've been slammed into the hay all over again.

Only this time I don't get the skyrocketing air, the sweet rush of dizziness. This time it just feels like I've hit a clump of bird shit; and it's all over my face, all over my body, all over my soul.

I drop the gnome. It doesn't break. Thank god, it doesn't break.

And when I look up, it's Mark that I see, because Petal's already halfway up the stairs, running to her own fall. It's Mark that I see, and I can't help but think that this is all his fault. All his fucking fault.

"What happened?" The words tumble from my mouth. Fumbled, bungled. They sit between us in the hay. "What happened to Amy?"

He shakes his head, the ends of his blue scarf twitching. "You've asked me a million times," he says. "I've already told you. I don't know, Ella. I don't."

The questions, the questions that drive me, they're loaded on the tip of my tongue now. I fire them off. Bullets. "But you must know where I was that night? Where she was? Why I can't remember anything?"

His back tenses, as if there's some kind of weight strung across his shoulders. "I don't," he says, sliding the words out the side of his mouth. "I wish I did, but I don't." He smiles. It's supposed to be a sad smile, but his lips slide too far to the left.

Sideways smile. Sideways smile and sideways words.

15

It's what I get every time I ask Mark what happened.

"Okay," I say, even though I don't believe him for a second.

Because Mark and Amy were so, so close. *AmyandMark. MarkandAmy.* She would have stayed near him the entire night. She thought all his shitty jokes were brilliant.

"Okay," I say again. I've already fought with Mark about this. Once. Twice. Three times. I can't go for round four; I'm too tired. And god, I'm also scared.

I don't want to lose another best friend.

"Ella," he says, "she never told any of us why. She was just in a bad place—"

"I have to go," I say. I don't want to hear this. I don't.

He runs a hand through his hair. No sparkle in his eyes, no smile on his lips, for once. "Ella, don't run away from the truth. Seriously, you can't blame yourself—"

I force a smile. "No," I say. "I really have to go. I have to be somewhere."

"Where?"

It's childish, but I don't want to tell him about the volunteer work I'm doing. Not when he won't tell me where I was that night, what happened, how the fuck Amy's body wound up broken, curling through the weeds in front of my garden gnome.

"Just somewhere."

And then I'm outside. I'm outside, heading down the

path that leads from the barn back to town, toward the child care center.

I turn back every few steps to take in the barn. It's built from this red cedar wood that glistens like dried blood in the sun. There's no door. Its entrance is an empty space in the wood, a black hole.

My best friends are on the other side of that black hole.

I hear Petal call "Geronimo!" Hear her scream filled with fear and exhilaration.

And suddenly I want nothing more than to be back in that barn. Falling. Slamming into the ground so hard that I think my teeth might rattle out of my mouth.

Because sometimes when I fall, I don't just remember. I forget.

Chapter Three

I TEXT AMY AS I HEAD DOWN A STREET LINED WITH BEAUTI-
ful mansions.

Walking the mean streets of Sherwood.

Hit SEND. Even though I know that her number's been
disconnected for fifteen days now, that some automated
message will arrive in a second telling me there's been an
error.

I hit SEND because this is one of those hundreds of
moments each day when I just want to tell her something.

About how Brittany Evans is making up shit about Liz
Wu hot-wiring a car last Saturday, which supports our the-
ory that she's a compulsive liar. About how in the morning
on the way to school, Mark played that ridiculous song
about being a fucking beach ball again. About how that
weird boy was lying on the football field, arms windmilling
through the mud.

And I want to tell *Amy*, not Mark or Petal or anybody else. I want to tell Amy, because no one ever laughs as hard as she did. No one is as quick to smile. No one else comes back with perfect, witty commentary like she used to.

I slip my phone back into my pocket and keep trudging up the road.

The houses that line it—brown brick with ivy creeping up, up, up their sides—cast long shadows over me. This is the older part of Sherwood. In summer when I was a kid, I used to love coming here because of the way the sun swung down through the oak trees.

I used to love the smell of damp earth, the clean sting of the breeze. The way the moss scampered over the houses, almost making them part of the landscape, one with the trees.

But they've ruined it, ruined the whole feeling of this place. With the child care center.

It's at the end of the road—the used-car-salesman of buildings. Squat, ugly, and just a little bit greasy.

Sometimes I think parents, the world, the goddamn Man, wants children to grow up disenchanted; and that's why they create places like this. That, or the deteriorating vision of the older generations really needs to be taken more seriously.

Either way, the child care center is a pockmark on the face of this town.

I keep walking, and soon enough, I'm standing in front of the pockmark.

Wind gusts through the recently planted saplings, rustling up sighs. I sigh along with them.

I have to come here at least three days a week after school. Mom's insisting that I do it for six months. *Minimum.*

I know right now that's never going to happen.

God, there are actual *real*, *live* children here.

They play hopscotch on the footpath outside the center, mark up the pavement with smoky blue chalk lines, and hop-skip-jump their way over obstacles. Occasionally, they shriek at each other. I'm not sure how a game of hopscotch can be heated, but these kids are pulling faces like it's a matter of life and death.

My eyes wander up the steps. Oh, god. There's a girl with brown pigtails and glasses, her back heaving. She's crying.

I nearly turn and run.

I can't deal with crying children.

No. Way.

But I'm here now.

And it's this or therapy. That was Mom's ultimatum. After years of pretty much ignoring me, she creaked down onto my bed one night last week and spewed her parental concern all over me.

She asked me how I was doing; and when I said fine, she didn't budge. Spotted: the purple-yellow-blue bruise edging just beyond the reach of my T-shirt sleeve. Her eyes: Worried. Concerned. Anxious.

She sat up and spoke in a hard voice, a voice that hammered into me. She gave me the ultimatum. "See my shrink, Ella, or do something wholesome," she said. "You need to pull yourself together." And I couldn't help but laugh, because for the past month all I've been trying to do is tear myself apart.

She gave me a stare that was cold. And then she told me that she knew how much I hated Roger—her shrink—so she'd organized some volunteer work at the local child care center for me and wasn't that so, so wonderful.

Yeah. Fantastic. Whoop-de-doo.

Now I stare up at the center's bland concrete facade. Take a deep breath.

Can'tdothis can'tdothis can'tdothis. But I walk around the hopscotch game, tread up the stairs. My feet carry me to the girl with the glasses. I drop my hand onto her shoulder. "Hey."

She looks up, choking for air, smashing her hands into her eyes to get rid of her tears. I decide not to embarrass her by asking about the tears, even though it's dead obvious from the red-rimmed eyes what her favorite after-school activity is.

21

"I'm Ella," I say. "I'm new here—can you show me the ropes?"

My new friend, Casey, knows next to nothing about the ropes. She takes me to the front desk and points at a wiry woman watering a potted plant.

Her back's turned, and she holds the watering can with lazy fingers. It doesn't seem as if she's at all worried about the room stretching out behind her. About the children eating at the low, colorful tables a few feet away. About the others, red markers in hand, drawing on the blackboard that hangs on the back wall. About the boy with brown hair lingering by the backpacks who has unzipped way more of them than he can possibly own.

"She knows," Casey says. "She's in charge."

How comforting.

"Thanks," I say, smiling at Casey before attempting to get the woman's attention. "Um, excuse me—"

She turns. The expression on her face makes me take a step back. It's the same look my dad used to give me when I was younger and had walked into his study. Like she wants nothing more than to annihilate me.

"I'm—"

"I know who you are," she says. The broken glass in her voice threatens to cut my skin.

"Casey," she continues, "why don't you go outside? Maybe play with the other children?"

"But—"

"They're about to play a nice game of duck, duck, goose outside, dear. I'm sure you'll love it."

Wiry Woman's voice is too sweet: condensed milk mixed with poison.

Casey moves away from us on uncertain feet, feet that trip and tumble over each other. She nearly slams into the floor, but grabs the door frame just in time.

Another kid who's sitting at a tiny table eating a salad and messing with an Etch A Sketch throws a half-eaten cherry tomato at Casey. It pings off her stomach. The girl who threw it laughs and laughs and laughs as it rolls away over the blue carpet and gets lost in a dark corner.

Forgotten. Just like this incident will be, even though I can tell from her pursed lips that Wiry Woman saw exactly what went down.

Casey doesn't say anything, either. She just pull, pull, pulls at the end of her pigtail and continues on. Out the door.

It's becoming apparent to me why Casey's favorite after-school activity is crying.

I glare at Wiry Woman, but she's too busy playing with paperwork to notice. I clear my throat.

Flash. Gray-lightning eyes behind blue-rimmed spectacles. "Be patient," she snaps at me. Then she dumps the mass of paper on my side of the desk. "This," she says, "is for you to fill out."

I don't reply, because something about this woman pisses the hell out of me. I'm determined to give her nothing but silence.

I shuffle forward. Take a look at the paperwork. It's pretty standard stuff. They want to know my name, my age, where I live, that kind of shit. I guess to make sure that I'm "suitable" to work here.

Probably should have done that before they told Mom they'd hire me.

I'm still carrying the soggy *Gazette* around, so I plunk it down on the tabletop and pull the sheaf of paperwork toward me. But now Wiry Woman's staring at it, at the article about Amy.

"Your best friend, right? She's dead."

My head snaps up, but I'm too stunned to reply because her voice is blank. The kind of blank that people twist around anger, hatred. I can feel my skin getting warm and red. Tomato soup on the boil.

Eventually, I manage to nod. "Yeah," I say.

"She was a horrible person."

"What?"

I don't know what I was expecting. Sympathy, maybe.

24

That typical, old-woman cluck of the tongue. Something about wasted youth, fragility, the preciousness of life. Not this. Anything but this.

"You heard me," Wiry Woman says. "She was a horrible person."

I take the time to read the name tag pinned to her floral blouse, because seriously, how many people who wear fucking floral blouses are this rude? It reads HEATHER PATON.

"It takes one to know one," I tell the woman. "Didn't anyone teach you not to speak ill of the fucking dead?"

Slam. She thuds her hand against the desk. A page skids off it, onto the blue carpet. "Language. There are *children* here," she says significantly, looking at a nearby cluster of tables where kids are eating.

I clench my fist, digging my fingernails into my palm. *Don't punch her, don't punch her, don't punch her.*

Fists uncurl. Nostrils flare. "I don't care—"

"Well, you'd better," she says, her sharp voice swiping across my words. "Because let me tell you, the only reason you're here is because your mother called and begged me. She's donating—well, she's donating a lot for you to be here."

Mom paid off this woman to *let* me do fucking volunteer work?

Typical.

"Listen," I say, "you don't even know me—"

"Ella Logan." Wiry Woman, Heather, spits out my name. "I know who you are," she says. "I know *exactly* who you are. You're the girl who bullied my son every day until he snapped. You and your best friend. Both of you are horrible people."

Some of the flames burning inside me douse. I lick my cracked lips. "Who is your son?"

"Oh, god," she says with a short laugh. "So many victims that you can't even remember him? Peter. His name is Peter."

Oh.

I do remember him. Clearly. He had a crush on Amy in ninth grade, right about when she started going out with Mark. Amy hated everything about him. From his leather boots to his shaggy, blond, shoulder-length hair to his nose ring. She hated the way he laughed and the way he spoke with his hands.

He didn't seem like a bad guy. Not really. But Amy had to send him a message. She had to tell him to back off somehow.

So one day we started laughing every time he spoke in class. Laughing like someone had just said the funniest thing in the world. Laughing, clutching our stomachs like they were about to burst open. And it

26

But the words evade me. I leave the unfinished paperwork and head for the same doorway Casey passed through earlier.

I spot the half-eaten tomato on my way out. It sits beneath shadows and a finely woven spiderweb.

The boy from the football field is there, on the other side of the door. The boy who danced his arms through thick mud and opened himself up to a lightning bolt. I know it's him because even though he's not splattered in mud anymore—must have gone home to change or something—I recognize his hair, the fluttery flames that twist away from his head.

I'm almost surprised that trails of black-gray smoke don't curl out from the ends of his hair. I'm almost surprised that he doesn't blow up everything around him with all the tension I saw earlier today. He's a bit of a bomb, this guy.

So why the fuck is Explosive Boy here? Why the fuck is he sitting in a circle with a bunch of kids surrounding him?

I'm heading toward the bench in the corner because I don't want to talk to anyone right now. I want to slump onto the rusty old bench with its peeling green paint and run my hands over my face and find stray eyelashes and blow them off the pads of my fingers, wishing with all my heart that Amy will come back to life and reply to the text messages I've sent.

But Casey sees me before I can hide away. She waves at me, small hand swaying back and forth, back and forth, back and forth. "Ella!"

And her face is brighter than the fog lights on Mark's car, Cherry Bomb. And the other kids, they look like sharks from this distance. To them, her brightness must taste like blood. To them, she must be a meal waiting to happen.

And maybe I really am sorry about Peter. Maybe that's why something about Casey's face makes me move. I wave back and walk over.

The new kid, Explosive Boy with his firebrand hair, is teaching them origami. Using long pianist's fingers to twist a blue scrap of paper into a crane. The kids are fascinated. They give him their undivided attention.

So now he's Explosive Boy the Kid Whisperer.

What the fuck?

"Tristan, Tristan!" one little boy says, drumming a chubby hand against the elbow of Explosive Boy's beaten leather jacket.

"Yes?"

"Can we play duck, duck, goose?"

"Man," Explosive Boy says. He's got just the right amount of air in his voice to sound casual, approachable.

Just the right amount of flame to sound warm. "Heath, I haven't played that game in over ten years—"

He looks up at me. I look down at him.

His eyebrows snap together for a second. Then he gets to his feet and smiles at me. A maple syrup smile. I back up, because Explosive Boy isn't meant to have a smile like that. But he extends a hand and catches mine, stops me from backing up any farther. Up and down, he moves our knotted hands in some kind of screwed-up handshake.

He smells of gunpowder. Maybe he's an arsonist. Probably my kind of guy.

"I'm Tristan," he says. "I'm volunteering here. Guess you are, too. What's your name?" He's smiling at me.

He probably thinks I'm going to be his new best friend or something.

"Ella. And you look more like an E to me," I say. E for Explosive Boy. E because I like having the power to rename him whatever I want to.

Something shifts behind his eyes. He drops my hand faster than my mother drives. He drops my hand at 180 mph.

The warmth's gone from his hazel eyes. And then he's running his hand through his hair; and I see fingernails chewed down to the quick, and I think *This is more like it.* This is more like the Explosive Boy I was expecting.

He gives me a frost-burn look before turning around.

"Okay, guys. Heath's going to get his wish. Let's split into two groups and play duck, duck, goose. Ella,"—he jerks a thumb at me as if I'm as noteworthy as a carton of milk—"will lead one, and I'll lead the other."

The little boy with the brown hair, Heath, jumps up and down and punches his tiny fists through the air. "Yessss," he says. It's so cute it hurts to watch.

E's taken a few steps away from me, his back purposefully turned. An ocean of kids already swims around him.

I'm a lonely island. There are three kids in my group, and they've placed a healthy distance between themselves and me. My bitch-face must make me relatively childproof. Halle-fucking-lujah.

Casey's stepping toward me now, but she hesitates inches from where E's standing.

"What's up?" he asks her with that maple syrup smile.

She's silent, but her dark eyes are looking at me. Looking at me and then looking back at Tristan. Is she going to sidle into the space beside him and join the dark side? For a moment I'm so sure that she will, but then she says "Nothing" to him and bounds over to my side.

"Hey," I say, somehow relieved, even though she's the child here. *She's* supposed to be relieved to have *me*.

"Are you going to be a duck or a goose?" It's such a casual question, or at least it should be. But her tone is probing, ponderous. As if she's just asked me whether I'm

other children watching her, she throws back her head and lets the sound pour forth.

And suddenly it makes sense. Why I've been so annoyed at the other kids for treating her badly. Why I've been wanting to punch and kick and make Casey's world safe.

Because her laugh? It's pure joy and adrenaline. It's heartbreak and happy-dance. Beautiful glass crystal shattering in the air.

It's *Amy's laugh*.

I cry.

Not with the children all around. Not as a sitting duck.

I cry in an alleyway behind the center after everyone's gone home. A place hidden from all eyes. The last two hours with Casey have been torture. She is Amy, age ten, in so many ways. From the pigtails to the slight chubbiness to the isolation to the silver-framed glasses to the laugh with so much freaking life in it.

I wrap my arms around myself, lean into the wall. My shadow streaks up the alleyway, long and lanky, beneath a perfect blue sky with streaks of orange sunset.

Fuck it. Fuck this day for being lovely.

I kick an empty milk carton off a pile of trash. It hits the wall at the same time that the door next to me crashes open.

Explosive Boy.

Seriously? Did he really have to decide to leave the center through the back entrance that Heather told me no one ever uses? I run my sleeve over my face hoping to catch some tears, to hide them away in the blue material.

I stare at the filthy ground, at the bird shit clumped around my sneakers. He can't see me crying. He can't.

"Um," he says. "Hey."

Why doesn't he just go away? Why does he have to stand there watching me like some kind of sadist?

Maybe he doesn't know I'm crying. Doesn't matter. I ignore him, hoping he'll pick up the hint. *Fuck off, E.*

The sound of his footsteps echo through the alley-way. I breathe a sigh of relief, thanking god he's gone. But then I smell gunpowder. And I realize he's standing close, too close. I try to back up, but I'm already against the wall.

He digs around in his pocket, produces a packet of tissues, and holds them out to me. When I make no move to take them, he shoves them at me. I can't see anything except white tissues and blue packaging. It's right up in my face, the plastic about to crackle into my nose.

I take the tissues. More to regain my vision than anything else.

E step, step, steps away. He heads back through the door, hands stuffed in his pockets. But he turns around just before the door closes, and I can see it twisting his face. Pity. Then he's gone.

He pities me. He fucking pities me.

I slam my shoulders into the wall behind me, let the pain rip through my already-bruised body. Because no one is supposed to pity me. *No one*. Especially not this boy, this strange, intense boy.

Ever since Amy died, I haven't been myself. I haven't been the girl with energy and anger burning up inside her all the time. Instead, I've been the girl with apathy simmering in her stomach.

But the little pity party E just threw me? It rekindled my flames.

I stuff the packet of tissues into my pocket.

Oh, I'm definitely going to light Explosive Boy's fuse.

Chapter Four

"*C*AN I COME IN, HONEY?"

Mom's already in my room, so I don't know why she's bothering to pretend she respects my personal space. I'm sure as hell not bothering to reply. I draw the covers up around me.

Morning silence slumbers over us, broken only by my mother's sharply drawn breaths. They're as crisp as her business suits.

"How was yesterday?" she asks.

"Wholesome."

"How was it really?"

I press my face more deeply into the pillow. The cotton sticks to my face, making it difficult to breathe. When I finally raise my head to gulp down air like a dying goldfish, the covers fall off me. There's no getting out of this conversation now.

I twist to face her. She's mostly a slim, long silhouette

standing beside my empty bookshelf; but morning light falls in dribs and drabs across one side of her face, illuminating half of her aristocratic nose and one bright brown eye. She's applied her makeup so perfectly that it looks as if she has no crow's feet.

"So," she says. "How was it?"

"Pretty bad," I lie. Because really, it wasn't too bad. "But it's there or sitting with Roger, right?"

"Right," she says, sweeping some of the dust off my bookshelf and straightening her suit. "I'm so glad I organized this for you, honey."

I nearly snort. *Organized*. She fucking bribed Heather Paton to let me volunteer. But I let it slide, because it's the morning and I could be—should be—sleeping right now. Besides, no one ever wins arguments against my mother.

Sometimes I think that's why Dad stopped coming home.

"I'll see you when I get back," she tells me, heading toward the doorway. She pauses, turns to me with this expression that's softer than my pillow. It's not an expression I'm used to seeing on my mother's face, and it leaves me more disoriented than the ray of light slinking through the shutters.

I squint to avoid blindness.

When I look back at the doorway, Mom's gone.

"Yeah," I call after her. "See you."

But that's a lie, too. I never see my mother in the evenings. She gets home from work so late, and she just crashes. And I get home from school, or wherever I've been after school, a mess. Wanting to throw myself off the third story of the barn, cry my eyes out, or climb up onto my roof and watch the garden, the space where the gnome used to sit.

Sometimes I want to do all three at once.

I tend to keep my bedroom door locked, and she tends to keep her bedroom door shut.

There are locks on our mouths, too. We never talk about Dad. We've adopted a don't ask, don't tell policy. She knows where he is—I'm certain that she knows where he's disappeared to for the past few weeks—but she's sealed away the words, and I don't care enough to crack her open and pry them out.

The number of appearances Dad makes at home has been thinning for a while now. Over the past few years he's been drifting away from his trophy house, the wife who was supposed to be a trophy but who liked her work too much, and his fuckup of a daughter who couldn't get anything right: not the schoolwork, or the boys, or the basketball. It was after I quit basketball in tenth grade that Dad and I really stopped talking, that Dad really stopped coming home.

But I get it. I mean, what's here for him? A kitchen island that all of us sit around together—but apart. Gleaming stainless steel appliances, wide-screen TVs, rich carpets, and an ache. An ache of what was supposed to be in this house, the dreams that were meant to be lived out here but never will be. All of those dreams got buried in our front garden when Amy jumped that night. And our house became even more tomb-like.

So I won't ask Mom where Dad's gone to, because I know why he's gone, and that's enough.

I get out of bed, for the same reason I have each and every morning since Amy died: to escape this place. To escape the silences, the shadows and dust. The hollow spaces. Wandering through my house, it's clear that a family used to live here. Once upon a time.

God knows where they've gone.

Brittany Evans tracks me down outside my locker. She thinks we're friends or something. I don't know what to tell her. I guess we are, if breathing the same polluted air daily a friendship makes. Her lunch table is just a few over from mine. We go to the same school, attend the same parties.

She was there that night. At my seventeenth birthday party. I'm pretty sure it's why the news of Amy's death spread so quickly. Why, when I returned to school after a

41

week, the first group of freshmen I passed were discussing how Amy had done it. Whether she'd used a rope or a gun or a kitchen knife or a bungee jump without the bounce.

It's something I haven't been able to fathom since Amy died. How people, especially people who knew her, could take the ending of her life and make it another piece of gossip. How they could use it for shits and giggles along with the celebrity fuckup of the week.

"So," she says. This is how Brittany always begins a conversation. "So, have you heard about the new boy?"

She's probably referring to Explosive Boy, but I haven't heard about him. I've heard from him. "No," I say, dumping all my books into my locker.

Brittany snakes an arm past me and picks up one of the books. *Hamlet.* "You have English Lit first period on Tuesdays, right?"

She knows my timetable. How very fucking disturbing. "Right," I say, taking the book from her and tossing it back into my locker. "What do you want, Brittany?"

Up go the hands. *Stop right there, thank you very much, Queen Bitch Ella.* That's what they seem to say, but that's not what Brittany's saying. She's saying, "Whoa, just wanted to talk to an old friend." I wait for more, because Brittany Evans never wants to just talk to an old friend. "And

I was wondering whether you'd heard about the new boy. Tristan? He's a senior, red hair, kinda cute?"

I shake my head, even though it's obvious she's talking about E.

"Well," she continues. "I don't know, but I've heard some weird stuff—he's into *burning* things, Ella. Shawn Robson saw him give this Bunsen burner the creepiest look in chemistry. And he smells of gunpowder, you know?"

"Right."

"Liz Wu said she saw him yesterday rolling around in the middle of the football field in all that mud. She thinks he was trying to wash away the smell of the gunpowder or something. Maybe he killed someone."

I roll my eyes, even though I smelled the gunpowder myself yesterday. "Maybe he just smokes weird shit," I say.

Brittany shakes her head. "No," she says. "Liz swears she smelled gunpowder. What are you going to do, Ella?" She pushes her glasses up her nose, brown eyes wide, shining with excitement.

Brittany wants me to break this guy because she thinks he's explosive. She wants to see sparks. I want to break this guy because he dared give me his fucking pity. The whole thing is so ironic that I can almost taste the metal.

I'm wearing the same pair of jeans as yesterday. Explosive Boy's packet of tissues is in the pocket. What I'm going to do is make sure that before the day is out he needs those tissues way more than I do. But letting Brittany in on that would be like giving away a war plan to the entire school.

So I stare her down. "What are *you* going to do?"

I slam my locker shut and walk away.

Chapter Five

*E*XPLOSIVE BOY HAS THE NERVE TO SMILE AT ME WHEN he walks into English Lit. Has the nerve to sit down directly in front of me. Has the nerve to claim Amy's seat.

The smell of gunpowder is even more intense than yesterday.

I subtly flip him off by trailing my middle finger over the bridge of my nose.

Mark, who's sitting beside me, lets out a yelp of laughter. "Being your usual friendly self today, I see," he says.

I shrug and kick my feet into the back of Explosive Boy's chair. Amy's old chair. *Knock, knock, knock, E. Who's there?*

No one, apparently, since he doesn't even turn around to look at me.

Maybe the rumors about me, about the crazy bitch I am, have reached him, and he no longer wants anything to do with me. Too bad. He gave me his pity and his Kleenex, so I'm going to give him hell.

By plunging him headfirst into a Pick Me Up.

Honestly? I've been looking for someone like this for a while. Pick Me Ups are getting boring. We could use another member, an explosive member, to heat things up.

I open my mouth to whisper-shout this to Mark, but our English teacher, Mr. Woodson, walks in before I can get a word out. Teachers. They're all masters of the art of bad timing.

Woodson sees Mark and me sitting one row from the front, and raises his eyebrows. "Miss Logan, Mr. Hayden, how lovely of you to join us today."

"No problem," I say sweetly, even though the acid in his words doesn't escape me.

We've missed the past few classes. Just didn't feel like being here. Once we came and walked out halfway through. If it was anyone else, Mr. Woodson would have kicked them out of his AP Lit class into a crappier intermediate one.

But it's *us*.

Before Amy died, we were the ultimate word nerds. Slinging Shakespeare quotes back and forth between us. Arguing over whether or not Freud was relevant or irrelevant or just a fucking misogynistic bastard.

Before, it was Mark and Amy and Petal and I in this

class. All four of us. And then Amy killed herself, and Petal hid away for so long that she was too behind to rejoin the class when she returned to the world of the living.

Now it's just Mark and I. And two empty seats in our row. Until E came along, that is.

Woodson claps his hands together. "So, if you guys read the notes on Aristotelian tragedy I handed out last week, you'll be able to pick up on how that structure is operating in the scenes we're about to read. Hamlet is going to—"

I tune out. I don't even have any paper, any pens to pretend to take notes with. Shit, I really am letting my act slide.

I snatch a pen off the table in front of Mark, steal his notebook, and flip it open to a blank page.

The guy in front of you. Check him out.

Mark grins and scribbles furiously before sliding the notebook back to me.

UNFORTUNATELY, I'M JUST NOT COOL ENOUGH TO BE GAY. ELLA, YOU SHOULD KNOW I DON'T CHECK OUT DUDES. I CAN'T GOSSIP ABOUT HOW CUTE HIS BUTT IS WITH YOU. GO FIND PET.

It's such a ridiculous comment that I snort with laughter. And then grab an eraser from his pencil case and throw it at him. Our shoulders shake and shake and shake with silent laughter, and for a moment I feel totally okay. For one second everything is whole.

And then I wonder whether I should be feeling this way with Explosive Boy sitting in Amy's seat.

And once that thought has wormed its way into my mind, the laughter falls out of my mouth.

Mark's shoulders keep on quivering, but I'm letting red pen bleed all over the notebook again.

He could play Pick Me Ups with us? The new kid. I shove the notebook toward Mark.

Now I've got his attention. His brows get tangled with each other, and he lets out a soft, low whistle. He slides a single word out the corner of his mouth. "Why?"

FRESH MEAT.

He draws a smiley face next to that. Writes, *You CANNIBAL.*

"Seriously, though," he says, keeping his voice low. "Why?"

I shrug. "For fun. To shake things up a bit."

Me? I don't bother to keep my voice down. My words have shattered the English teacher's preciously cultivated silence.

Woodson looks at me and sighs. He opens his mouth, then thinks better of it because I'm still the kid with a dead best friend. I'm still fucked-up Ella Logan, and it's still better to leave me the hell alone.

"I think he could be up for it," I say.

Mark flicks his eyes over to Explosive Boy. Sizes him up and nods. His lips curve. He's impressed.

He leans toward me. "Do you want him in?" His words are whisper-quiet. I doubt anyone but me, and maybe Explosive Boy, is close enough to catch them.

I nod.

Mark gives the new kid another appraising look. His mouth twitches up at the sides. Grimace. "Yeah, okay, he might be up for it," he whispers. But he's giving me this look. This pointed stare. It's all *why the hell would you do that?*

He pulls the notebook over. Scribbles. Slides it back to me.

Is HIS BUTT THAT CUTE?

I laugh and shake my head. Even if Explosive Boy had the kind of face that looked as if it had been broken into halves, quarters, eighths, and then pasted back together again with the average glue stick, I'd want him in.

No one's butt is that cute.

THEN WHY?

I tap my nose. For me to know and Mark to never find out.

Mr. Woodson begins casting people into various roles so we can reenact *Hamlet*. Go Shakespeare, way to write a tragedy that people willfully, stupidly repeat over and over again throughout the ages.

I sneak a hand toward Explosive Boy's back. Tap him—well, more like punch him, actually, because taps aren't my style.

To his credit, he doesn't even jump.

I can tell I'm going to like this guy. Which is too bad, because I'm also going to break him.

He spins to face me. "Yeah?"

Voice like earth mixed with gravel. The soil of my garden that Amy crashed into.

And suddenly my face wants to crack like a mirror under the pressure of seven years of bad luck. But I force my lips to twist, my brows to lift.

"You up for it, then? Pick Me Ups?"

He turns around and stares at me. Hard. As if he thinks his hazel eyes can bore holes into my skin and stop me from staring right back at him. Not happening. Explosive Boy doesn't scare me.

Not one little bit.

"What are they?" he says eventually. "What are Pick Me Ups?"

We have an audience now. It's as if I'm a magnet, and everyone in this room is made of metal. And given the horrible things we do to one another while trapped in this building, most of us probably do have hearts made of iron and steel and aluminum.

I lean toward Explosive Boy. Close. Closer.

Our cheeks graze against each other's. If I move just a little bit more, my lips will brush across his earlobe.

"They're orgies," I stage whisper.

Everyone hears it. They draw a collective breath, and it's deadly quiet for a moment. By tomorrow Brittany Evans will be telling the whole school that the new kid and I are doing it, covered in hay down at the barn. With Mark and Petal in supporting roles, of course.

"Seriously?" E says. He's still speaking at normal volume. It doesn't fit with his unintimidating presence around the kids yesterday.

"Yes." I pull out my best Sexy Voice.

He looks totally unimpressed. "You're so full of shit," he says. But I can hear the doubt in his voice, the little question mark in his words.

Am I really bullshitting?

Of course. I'm always bullshitting. But he doesn't know that.

"Well, then, don't be a curious bitch. You don't know what Pick Me Ups are until you try them. That's just how it works."

There isn't really a rule about secrecy. I made it up. Because if he knew what he was getting himself into beforehand? He'd never do it. No matter how Explosive he is. And I need him to say yes right now.

I wait for his reaction. Inside, I'm holding my breath.

I examine my nail, flick away a piece of dirt. My features are like cardboard: not a scrap of emotion or color.

This is how I play the game. He can't know I want anything from him because then he'd have leverage. I'm the only one who's supposed to have leverage.

But he's still in my face. So close that his breath, surprisingly clean and fresh, tickles my cheek. I notice the packet of Tic Tacs in his upper pocket. He's waiting for me to break, but I stare at him unflinching, my blinking and breathing even.

Finally, he leans away from me, taking the smell of mint and gunpowder with him. I notice his fingers burrowing into the pockets of his jacket. Wonder what he's hiding there. Matches? A knife? Or just his fingers?

The class is riveted. Their saucer-wide eyes make me want to purr with contentment. Who needs to study Shakespeare when you've got love and lust and death—and promised orgies—unfolding right before your very eyes?

E's lazy drawl cuts through whatever the English teacher's saying. "I'm in."

Chapter Six

"MISS LOGAN," MR. WOODSON CALLS THE SECOND THE bell rings. "Remain after class, please. I need to speak to you."

Most people get saved by the bell. I get burned by it.

There's a flurry of movement as everyone packs their books. They bob out of the classroom one by one. Blond, brunette, brunette, redhead, blond.

Mark gives me a comforting punch on the arm. "I'll wait for you outside," he says. He grabs his stuff and leaves.

I get up and cross the short distance between where I'm sitting and where Mr. Woodson's standing. Then I just wait. And wait. Pretend that the mahogany wood of his desk, with Sherwood High's crest carved into it, is the most fascinating thing in the world.

He's the one who wanted to see me. I'm not going to make it easier for him by initiating the conversation.

He rocks back, peers at me seriously for a second, then says, "Ella, how are you doing?"

What am I supposed to say?

Shit. I feel like shit all the time.

That's not what he wants to hear. That's not what anyone wants to hear. Because that's the kind of world we live in, and that's the kind of town Sherwood is.

We're all supposed to be fine all the fucking time.

"I'm okay," I say, trying to keep my tone upbeat. I hope I've got that bright-eyed, hopeful, entirely-too-young look on my face. It's the type of look that could get me out of trouble right now.

"So why haven't you been coming to class?"

The look obviously isn't working.

I turn over possible answers in my mind.

Because it's boring. Because I prefer carrying out secret masochistic pastimes. Because my own life is so full of drama right now that I don't need Shakespeare as well.

Because.

I shrug. Don't say anything.

"I understand—"

"No, you don't."

I'm not sure where these words come from. But they pop out of my mouth. They sit between us, an ugly truth. I'm sure every teenager on the planet has thought this at some point, but I really don't think anyone understands this world.

It's a senseless place full of senseless people.

"Well, regardless," he says, not looking so convinced, "I have to tell you that if you miss any more classes, I'm going to have to inform the school and your parents. You can't remain in my class if you aren't going to show up."

Why, god? Why did you stick me with the one teacher in the entire school who gives a fuck?

"That's unfair," I say. I think it's mandatory that I utter this line, play up the role of teenage miscreant. "Look, you're not doing anything to Mark, and we've missed all the same classes."

Woodson frowns. "I think you know perfectly well, Miss Logan, why I'm not dealing with Mr. Hayden like this. If I have to drop him from my class—"

He loses his scholarship.

Of course.

"That's not what I meant. I'll—" I chew my lip. I'd be lying if I said I'd start attending classes again. Not that I have a problem with lying. Problem here is that it would be too goddamn obvious. As soon as my seat's empty tomorrow morning, Woodson will know I was messing with him.

And he'll call my parents. And Mom will—I actually don't know. Maybe she'll prescribe another Wholesome

55

Activity for me to do. The truth is, it doesn't matter whether I attend school or not because, with my parents, there won't be any real consequences.

A smile edges its way onto my face. I shoo it away. Straight face. "What happens if I keep up this way?"

"You get moved into a normal literature class. You flunk. Do you want to graduate, Miss Logan?"

Frankly, my dear English teacher, I don't give a damn.

Once upon a time I did.

Last year, sophomore year, I was Ella Logan. I was going to ace school. I wouldn't do as well as Mark, who was all set to become valedictorian; but the Ivy League would admit me, and I'd tell them to stick their offers up their asses and go to NYU. I'd get away from suburbia and meet new people. There'd be life everywhere. There'd be shouts and whispers and sobs all in a single second, and I'd be able to see it all. Soak it all in.

More than anything, that was what I wanted. It was The Dream. I was going to get away from Sherwood. I was going to get away from rich people and my parents and the rest of it.

And once upon a time, Amy was coming with me.

Then it all ended unhappily ever after.

I don't want it. Not anymore.

But I don't tell Mr. Woodson this. Instead, I say, "I'll do my best."

Always easier to make an empty promise than it is to tell the truth.

"Stop skipping school," he says, a smile lighting up his wrinkled face, "and you can go back to being your old self."

And I nearly laugh, because he's so wrong. There's no way I can go back to being myself. Not when Amy will never move beyond being sixteen and young and stupid and stuck in this goddamn town.

She's dead. I know she's dead, but it feels as if she's still here. As if I have to stay with her.

"I'll do my best," I repeat, and force a weak smile. Then I grab my bag and bolt from the room.

I don't want to think about who I used to be. Or who I am. Or who I'm becoming.

I don't want to think about lost dreams.

Chapter Seven

EXPLOSIVE BOY IS STANDING BY THE WATER FOUNTAIN IN the tiny courtyard. I crunch over a bunch of twigs to get to him, enjoying the way his eyes grow wider and wider as I move toward him. They nearly pop out of his head when I grab his arm.

"Hi," I say. I pull him along, back inside the corridors of Sherwood High.

"What are you doing?" he asks. As if he's so fucking scandalized. But he follows me, and we're both needles threading our way through hallways crammed with students.

"Faster," I say, because Mark is waiting and I need to find Petal. "Let's go, let's go, let's go."

I'm aware that I sound like a drill sergeant, crazy and deranged. But I don't care. I've already fucked up first impressions with E by pulling that whole crying act. Now I get to be my screwed-up self.

"What are you *doing*?" he repeats.

"I'm dragging you through the corridors of your new high school. Consider it a tour."

"You're psycho."

"Well observed, Holmes."

To be honest, I'm not really sure why I've taken E barreling down this locker-lined hallway with me.

I was supposed to get Petal and meet Mark out in the parking lot. We were supposed to climb into Mark's car, Cherry Bomb, and drive straight to the barn.

E wasn't part of the plan. We were supposed to "Fuck him up another time," to quote Mark. He's eloquent, that boy.

But I saw E and I grabbed him. Guess this is his lucky day after all.

E says, "Could you just slow down for a second?"

"No."

He could pull away from me if he wanted. I'm not strong enough to hold him in place. He wants to be here, tagging along with me.

Drop the pretenses, Explosive Boy.

"What are you doing?"

"Looking for Petal."

I swerve down another corridor with about a million and one dust motes partying in it. Light filters through the stained glass windows. Red, blue, green, yellow. This is the older section of Sherwood High.

"Welcome to the rich-bitch part of our school," I tell Explosive Boy. Only the superwealthy kids receive the honor of a locker in this corridor. A locker beneath the gleaming mahogany boards that scream the glory of past students in gold lettering.

Standing here, you can practically feel the money of generations and generations of families. Almost all of them making worthless, but well-paid, contributions to society.

I stop moving when I'm standing beneath a board proclaiming the success of silver-screen actor Brody Ashton, who graduated in the class of '93. I stop moving because Petal's at the end of this corridor, crashing her head into a locker. She shouldn't be here.

She shouldn't be here because the locker she's in front of, it's not hers.

It's Amy's.

"Stay," I tell Explosive Boy.

"I'm not a dog."

But he listens to me like the loyal hound he is.

I march over to Petal. Tap my shoe against her shoe. "What are you doing?"

I'm using the worst tone in my repertoire. The Nothing tone. It's my voice pared down to the bone: no emotion, no feeling. But it sounds like a live wire, as if it could electrocute someone.

Then Pet looks at me, and I see the pain pulling her face apart. Her lip trembles and she collapses into me and I hold her. Her tears soak my T-shirt.

"What are you doing here?" I repeat more softly.

Does it have anything to do with what she and Mark aren't telling me?

A small earthquake rocks her shoulders. Her breaths come in gasps, knifing through her small frame.

"I just thought," she says, suddenly slamming her fist into Amy's locker. "I just thought that she might have left something in here. Some hint about why, how she was feeling—"

She breaks free of me. Slams her fist into Amy's locker again. And again.

Petal has never exactly been a pacifist. It's why Mark and I were so surprised when she shut herself away after Amy died. We thought she would fight the sadness. But Petal didn't leave her bedroom for two weeks aside from going to the bathroom. She didn't shower. She didn't speak to a soul. When she came out, she was ten years gaunter, ten pounds heavier; and she still barely spoke. At first. But Pick Me Ups breathed life back into her, brought back some of the fight that made her burn bright, bright, bright as if she were slightly mad.

And she's kicking the lockers now. Again, again, again, again, again. Kicking them so hard that her shoes

61

leave slight dents in the metal. It's extreme, even for Pet.

Her new skin, the one that makes her pirouette and attempt to steal from vending machines, peels away. And the truth about her, her heart and her guilt and her lies, is on display for the world to see. It's a shame that it remains unreadable, unfathomable to me.

She collapses, slides down against the cream-colored lockers. Her butt hits the rich, burgundy carpet, and she makes this sound. Halfway between a sob and a swear word.

"I just can't believe Amy would do this to us," she says. "I can't believe it."

I don't know what to say, because I can't believe it, either.

Silence. The dust motes float over us, flashing through the red light and then the green light. Petal's sitting in the blue light shredding her nail, as if she doesn't know what else to do.

"Mark and I are going," I say eventually, knowing that this is the only thing that might help her. "We're going to the barn."

I don't have to ask whether she's coming. She gets to her feet and follows me down the corridor. She throws me a weird look when Explosive Boy tags along with us. He gives her a wide berth. Even the grenade boy knows not to mess with Petal.

She watches him as we move through the corridors but doesn't say anything.

And then Petal's banging open the door that leads to the parking lot in that typical, melodramatic way that all of us have. Me included. Weak sunlight floats over E and me, who are left standing in the doorway.

E raises his brows at me. "Let me guess," he says. "You're all from rich-bitch central."

Because melodrama like this is reserved for the wealthy? Please.

Only Amy was from rich-bitch central. And maybe me. I could have a locker in the hallowed older section of Sherwood High. God knows I would if my father had stopped working long enough to realize that the administration hadn't already given me one. But this is my father and work we're talking about—they're going to the grave together—so that's highly unlikely.

If he ever comes home again, or if I discover where he's hiding, maybe I'll tell him. Maybe the injustice of my locker location will recapture his attention.

"Just get outside, okay?"

Mark stands next to Cherry Bomb. She looks just like she usually does—like a cherry-colored bomb. Yeah. We're really imaginative when it comes to naming things.

Mark looks like he usually does, too. Wonderfully idiotic. He's smoking a lollipop. The strawberry-colored sphere disappears into his mouth, pops back out again. Puff, puff, puff. Imaginary bits of lollipop smoke cloud the air.

"Mature, man."

Way. Too. Blunt. E.

Mark takes the lollipop out of his mouth. "Sarcasm is the lowest form of wit."

"Well, at least I'm witty," E returns.

And then Mark's moving toward E, his lollipop held aloft like some kind of sword, and I want to laugh so fucking hard. Instead, I put myself between them before my best friend perpetrates an act of lollipop violence. "Whoa, whoa, whoa, ladies. Too much testosterone."

Their laughs crack the air at the same time.

Ice breaks.

"Hey, man," E says. "I'm Tristan."

"We're all calling you E," I tell him.

"I don't—"

"You're E. Get the hell over it already."

E looks at Mark, trying his best to pull off a lost-puppy-please-help-me look. It doesn't work too well. E's ember hair is burning up against the white sky. He may be a grenade and a Kid Whisperer at the same time, but he's sure as hell no puppy dog.

"Don't look at me." Mark pops the lollipop back into his mouth, resumes his smoker act. "I still don't like you."

"What the *fuck* are you doing here, anyway?" Petal glares at Explosive Boy.

The broken ice freezes back over.

"I don't know," he says. "Ella just dragged me along."

Spotlight on me.

"Fresh meat, shaking things up," I say, rattling off the same excuses I gave Mark. Pet doesn't look convinced, and the glare she shoots me is so frosty it stings. Well, I can be a frigid bitch, too. "How about I fucking wanted to, Petal, okay? How about this is exactly like us wanting to start Pick Me Ups in the first place? Like you wanting to join in."

And just like that Petal looks as if I've snapped her in two. My words might sound inane on the surface, but if you dig a little deeper, the barbs will bite into your skin.

'Cause Mark and I invented Pick Me Ups without Petal.

We invented Pick Me Ups without Petal because she wasn't there. When she came out of her room, though, she saw things differently. She thought we'd spent the time bonding or something instead of just jumping off shit.

Now she feels like she's the outsider, the one on the

edge, even though it's she and Mark who are trying to drug me with their sideways words. Even though it's Mark and Pet who are holding back on me.

And now she's looking at me, and I want to tell her I don't mean it, any of it; but I won't. I can't.

I have to make her think it's real. Because I can't stand being the outsider, either.

"Okay," Petal says eventually. She pulls herself together, stretches a smile across her face. Runs her tongue across her front teeth, up over the edge of her lip. "So, what are we going to do with him?"

What *am* I going to do with him? Send him spiraling into a Pick Me Up, yes. But how?

"Yeah, what are you going to do to me?" E asks.

I ignore him.

My hands are moving now. Fingers threading their way through Mark's hair, disentangling today's hippie scarf. It's a lurid pink. *Snap. Snap. Snap.* I pull it taut between my fingers, grin at Explosive Boy.

He bends backward. "No," he says.

I step forward. Back he goes again.

"Come on, E," I say. And then, because lying is my favorite hobby, I add, "Pink's really your color."

"Where are you taking me?"

He's still tilted away from me.

"The b—"

"—nowhere important," I say, cutting off Mark. "You don't know until you get there, okay?"

"Not okay."

"Please. Your curious-bitch act is starting to annoy me."

"Your bitchy-bitch act is starting to annoy *me*," he says, but he stoops so I can wind the scarf over his eyes. Around, around, around. His nose and eyes vanish beneath the pink gauze.

When he's properly blindfolded, Mark opens Cherry Bomb's back door. Her familiar smell drifts to me. Boozy breath and late nights. Weirdly comforting.

"Ladies first," Mark says, gesturing to the door.

And Petal, without being told, immediately gets it and shoves E headfirst into the car. Our teamwork. It's a thing of beauty.

At least it would be if I didn't know they were lying to me about Amy.

"Ouch," Explosive Boy says, straightening himself on the backseat, on Cherry Bomb's landmine-of-holes upholstery. I watch as Explosive Boy dips his fingers into one of these backseat potholes. He snatches his hand back and flinches.

We howl with laughter.

But it dies out quickly. Probably because we're all thinking about how Cherry Bomb got those battle scars.

Amy. Amy did that. When she was so fucking smashed after this party in tenth grade. Grabbed a rock from somewhere and started slashing at the material, singing "Amazing Grace" beneath her breath the whole time.

Mark let her do it. He just kept driving, letting her destroy his car.

"Relax. It's stuffing," Petal says to Explosive Boy, who's still looking freaked-out. "You know the shit that comes out of cushions?" And that's Petal. The Petal I knew before Amy died, who was truly fucking concerned about people beneath her diamond exterior. She's not nice—none of us are nice—but Petal's the closest. And she has this amazing ability to compartmentalize. Pet can make mincemeat of some kid at school and then go out all weekend and fundraise for starving children in Africa.

She's the most loving misanthrope I've ever met.

She turns to me. "You sure you want this guy doing a Pick Me Up?"

I nod. The real reason I want Explosive Boy here goes beyond showing him I don't need his pity. The real reason he's here is purely strategic. It's because I need to figure out what Mark and Pet are hiding. And to do that, I need someone else to be the outsider, to push against us.

Push us together.

"I'm sure," I say. I nudge Mark. "Give me your keys."

"Why?" Shock and horror crash into each other on his

face, mangling his sweet baby-angel features.

"Seriously? *You* are afraid of *my* driving?"

There's a reason Cherry Bomb is such a bomb. That reason is Mark.

"Fine." He fishes the keys out of his jeans pocket. Tosses them to me. "But I'm riding shotgun to make sure you don't kill us all."

Petal winks at me. "Wonderful," she says, slipping into the backseat. "I get to guard our prisoner."

And then I'm hopping into the driver's seat. Putting my hands on the steering wheel. Turning the key in the ignition.

It's only when the engine roars to life and the entire car shakes around me that I figure out what I really want to do to E.

We're not going to the barn today.

Chapter Eight

I PULL OVER NEXT TO THE UNNAMED JUNGLE PARK AT THE edge of town.

We get out of the car, shoes scuffing the pavement, kicking mushroom clouds of dust into the air. Petal's holding Explosive Boy's elbow, making sure that he doesn't walk somewhere stupid, like back out onto the road. But she's looking at me. Looking at me as if I'm tearing her heart into halves, quarters, eighths, sixteenths. Shreds. As if I'm absolutely gutting her.

She thinks I'm going to keep us from Pick Me Ups today.

Where are we going? she mouths at me.

Trust me, I mouth back.

She digs her nails into Explosive Boy's elbow so hard he jumps. "Shit," he says. "What was that for?"

"Fun."

Mark, who's standing behind them, throws back his head and laughs.

I start walking toward the trees at the edge of the park. No one follows me. I slow down, wait for them. Nothing. The silent, dusty road breathes against my back. I pause. "Are you guys coming?"

"Coming where?" Mark says. "Let's get back to the car. Let's *go*."

Let's go. Let's get into Cherry Bomb and speed toward the barn. Let's speed toward our falls. Let's slam into the hay. Feel our pulses dim. And let's find that moment. That one moment in the fall that feels like absolution, like bliss, like a miracle's taken place inside our bodies.

But we're not going to the barn. Not today. Because jumping off shit in the barn isn't working anymore. I need to try somewhere new. Something else.

I stare at the trees. They're a mass of silvery brown, slurring and blurring into one another. Packed too close, like my mother packs her suitcases. But through a teensy-tiny gap between their trunks, I spot a rusty chain hanging from a green metal bar.

A swing set.

Once upon a time, this place must have been a real park. Tame and neat. Echoing with children's laughter. But I wouldn't be surprised if we found a lion prowling around here today.

Amy and I used to play here as kids, even though it was already wild by then. We used to play hide-and-seek. We'd curl ourselves into the weeds, hide away, and wait for the other to come looking.

I'd take hours finding Amy, inevitably losing other things in the process.

Lost: sandals, butterfly clip, jacket.

Found: Amy. Sometimes.

Now I look at the weeds and I wonder. I wonder whether, when she jumped off my roof and landed smack-bang in the curling, whispering weeds of my garden, she thought of this place.

The weeds we damn near lost ourselves in.

I think it's time for me to get lost again.

I jump over a clump of them. My sneakers sink into loosely packed soil on the other side of the weeds.

"Trust me," I say, out loud this time. "Do you have the gnome, Petal?" It's my way of easing their concern. There will be Pick Me Ups today. We still need our ref.

They're moving now, following me now, even though they don't look too happy about it.

"Yeah, I've got the gnome."

"What's the gnome?" E asks.

"The gnome?" Mark replies. "He's the one who's watching your every move." A laugh dances underneath the waves of his voice. Good vibrations.

"Sounds like some short commando dude or something." Explosive Boy seems genuinely confused.

Drama queens like me are allowed to be into orgies, new-kid hazing, and lying. But garden gnomes? Shit, even I think that's screwed up.

They're moving faster now. I wait for them to catch up, too scared to brave the park on my own.

Petal's nearly there now. She jumps over a clump of weeds and joins me under the cool shade of the trees. She's frowning, but she's staying with me. She and Mark are both staying with me. It feels good not to be alone.

I wonder how Amy felt. No one jumped after her.

"So where the fuck are we going, Ella Logan?"

Petal's mouth is close to my ear. She doesn't want Explosive Boy to hear this. Warm breath sliding into my eardrums, swirling with the sound of her words. "This most definitely isn't the way to the barn."

I lean close to Pet, feeling bad about my own stale breath. "We're going to the bridge."

"Are you crazy?" she hisses.

But Pet's always been bad at telling people not to do things that are unhealthy for them. She was born to be addicted to something, to everything. She loves her burgers and fries, her alcohol, her adrenaline rushes. Her Pick Me Ups.

And the bridge? The bridge is new and exciting. The

drop isn't far, but we'll be falling into water instead of bales of fluffy hay.

Hopefully, it'll be exciting enough that I'll get a memory back.

"You're crazy, too," I say, and continue marching through the weeds.

Mark rolls along with it, even though he still has no idea what's happening. He laughs and chants, "Left, right; left, right. You lead the way, Sarge Ella."

I hear E's soft cursing, the breathy fear in his voice. *That's right.* I smile to myself as I keep rhythm with Mark's chanting. *What the fuck have you gotten yourself into?*

Then I step onto the bridge. It squeaks beneath my feet like a seesaw. I can hear the bridge, feel it swaying beneath my feet.

I whoop.

On the edge of the bridge, E laughs. "Oh," he says as he steps onto the bridge. It creaks and crackles. "I know where this is."

None of us reply. We just step along the bridge. Normal people would tiptoe, afraid of sending the bridge crashing into the river. Mark and Pet don't tiptoe; but they both move lightly, on the balls of their feet.

I stride. I thunder like an elephant. Rust flakes away into the rushing white water below.

Clearly, I think as the metal jolts beneath my feet, *I'm not normal.*

"So, what, are you going to push me off the bridge? That's really not that crea—"

Mark grabs the back of E's jacket, lifts him a little, and shoves him over the safety railing. I watch Explosive Boy fall, watch his red hair blow up from his face, his black jacket buffeted by the wind. And that's when I realize the blindfold might not have been such a good idea.

Because if half his nose is covered, and he can't see—well, for me it would just mean a greater rush. But I'm in the habit of throwing myself off things. He's not. Fuck.

E hits the water with a splash. A belly flop into the rapids.

And now he's winded. Fuck.

At first Petal and Mark laugh; but then I point, and they notice how he's not struggling against the current. It's Mark's yell that splits the air, rips the blue sky in two, and drops the clouds around our heads.

The world crashes.

"Shit. What have we done? What have we done?" Petal says. "Fuck. I can't believe we did this again."

I think she's referring to Amy, but I'm not sure.

What aren't they telling me?

Can't focus on that now.

I tear off my jacket and stand up on the edge of the bridge. I pinch my nose, because that's how they always do it in the movies. And then I jump before Mark and Petal can grab me.

I fall like a vertical bullet. I'm expecting a memory to hit me, but nothing comes.

I crash into the river, my feet feeling as if they've shattered upon impact.

Cold and strong, the water surges around me. It doesn't take long for my feet to touch the muddy bottom.

I swallow my disappointment at not finding a memory and struggle up to the surface, struggle for breath, even though it would be so easy to let the water put me to sleep.

I can see E floating along with the current. It's a steady flow, but this river's washed out. It's not strong enough to make his limbs as useless as a puppet's. He might be in shock or something. Not being able to see or breathe right probably isn't helping.

Stroke, stroke, stroke. I speed up the current's flow. I'm beside him in what's not quite a minute, not quite a moment. *Three heartbeats' time,* Amy and I used to call it. But my heart's beating so fast, thudding bruises against my chest.

E's breathing bubbles, all of his air streaming out of him into the water. I put a hand on his shoulder. When that doesn't get his attention, I grab his head and pull him out of the water. He sucks in a deep breath and then the weight of his head, complete with soggy hair, becomes too much for me and I drop it again.

Bubbles in the water. White rushing above us.

White noise. White sound and fury.

My limbs are giving out. What's the point?

But I give it one last shot and pluck at the knot I tied in the scarf. It floats away, and I can see it from the corner of my eye. A pink dream, lost in the water.

I pull E and myself up for another breath, but as soon as we're down again he becomes a dead weight. I swim under him, trying to make eye contact, to threaten him into moving. But his eyes are closed. His skin is loose, his features slack. Unconscious.

Shit. There's no way I can force him to breathe for long enough. Acting as his personal ventilator is not going to work.

I need him to move fast.

I twist down in the water, spin my way through the current until I'm underneath him, and aim my knee at his pants. Bubbles spurt from my mouth. In this weird gravity, with my limbs floating everywhere, it looks something like ballet to me.

Who'd have thought that kneeing someone in the balls could ever be equated with beauty?

I'd like to say that my ballet-balls threat is what forces Explosive Boy to finally lift his body from the water, but I'm pretty sure he's still out cold.

Truth? The water releases us from its embrace. Cold mud slicks my back, and suddenly we aren't moving anymore. Suddenly, the sun is glaring at me and I'm not quite as wet.

E's eyes sludge open. He turns over, lifts himself off me—because with the water whooshing out from between us, he's practically on top of me. He sucks in sunshine and air.

I laugh. Triumph always makes me laugh. Living again and again and again always makes me laugh. But when I laugh, water shoots into my mouth and nose. It floods my lungs. The sun is so bright, and I can't help but think I'm dying.

I'm dying in a fucking puddle. On a sunny day.

I've one-upped Amy. She's going to be so pissed at me in heaven, or hell, or reincarnation. Wherever.

I splutter. Air slides into my mouth and nose in trickles. I hear voices above me, feel arms under me; but I'm just not getting enough air, and I sink into blackness.

Chapter Ten

*A*MY AND *P*ET AND *I* ARE SITTING AT THE KITCHEN TABLE.

Amy drinks her punch as if she's downing a shot and then scoops more out of the bowl we've hijacked.

"Let's play twenty questions," she says. "Every time you reveal something totally tragic about yourself, knock back some punch." She grins, golden skin lit by the soft light from the other room. "We all know it's spiked."

Because she spiked it.

Mark dances into the kitchen. He opens my fridge and grabs a beer. "What are you guys up to?"

"Twenty questions," I say. "You?"

"Some girl just offered to give me a striptease."

"Well, go have fun then," Amy says. She drinks half her punch in one gulp.

"Nah, Ames. I'll skip it for you, 'cause I'm a good boyfriend that way."

I give her the finger. "Drink some punch. Or I'm going to punch you."

Eight years, she's been one of my best friends. By now she must have realized that I'm far from perfect.

"Your turn, Marquis." Amy's been calling Mark that for the past couple of weeks. She's developed a thing for French novels or something. "So, if you could change one thing about your life, what would it be?"

"I'd have a hippie van instead of my crappy car."

"Be serious." She leans across the table, long limbs slightly lazy, slightly out of control. "Be serious," she repeats.

"Okay," he says. "Um. I don't know what I'd change, to be honest. I screw stuff up a lot; but to tell you the truth, I kinda like it that way."

I just keep staring at my punch. I wanted Mark to say that he'd give up the drugs if he could have had it any other way. Because his using went far beyond recreational last year, and it was fucking scary.

Something snaps, shattering glass, behind Amy's eyes. She looks away.

Petal laughs loud, because she's too drunk to even notice the tension. "Me, too."

"Your turn." Mark grins at her. "Who was your first kiss?"

This is a traditional question for Pet. We ask it every time. Every fucking time, and it still doesn't matter; the answer is still hilarious.

Petal wrinkles her nose. "Andy Burgerman."

"More like Booger Man," I say. He was this fat kid, famous for picking his nose.

We all shriek with laughter except Amy. She was a fat kid, too, all the way through middle school. People used to tease her. The words of school kids twined into the insults her parents were constantly throwing her way, and she fell apart.

Her fat dropped away as we went through middle school, and so did her spirit. She's gotten it back—her spirit—in the past couple of years. But she doesn't get that I'd love her, we'd love her, either way. Fat or thin or green and blob shaped.

It still hits her hard when we laugh at Booger Man. Because she imagines other kids, at some other kitchen table, putting their heads together and laughing about her.

And that thought makes me sick about what I've just said. I notice Mark's fingers curling around Amy's shoulder.

"I'm going to screw up the order," Pet says. Amy's quiet, staring at one of her black curls floating in the pink punch. She fishes it out and takes a sip. Punch spiked with vodka, and Essence of Amy.

She shakes her head, flicks away the bad thought. A few drops of punch still linger in that lock of hair.

"Back to you, Mark," Petal says.

He makes a face at her.

"What do you least want to admit to everyone at this table? Go around in order. What's the weirdest thing you've thought about Ella, Ames, and me?"

He turns to me and says, "Ella, in the seventh grade I had this dream about you."

"Stop right there! I don't want to hear about your horny seventh-grade dreams."

He laughs. "No, don't worry; it wasn't one of those dreams. You were riding a horse and singing 'Thriller' in a really high-pitched voice. And that's the weirdest thing I've ever thought about you."

"That's not too bad," I say. "But because you heard me singing 'Thriller' in your sleep; I think you need this." I grab a glass of punch and fill it. "Drink up."

He drinks and whoops, because he's Mark and that's what he does. "And you, Petal," he says. "You. Well, there was that time I thought you were considering becoming a stripper. Do you remember that?"

She slaps him lightly. "I do. But you were high, so I forgive you, my favorite stoner."

"Shut up. I'm not a stoner anymore."

"What about me?" Amy leans forward. Hair sliding into the pink punch again. Half submerged.

"You." Mark's voice drops. His words are a whisper in the dark, splashing into the punch. "I—I used to think that I liked you better when you were fat."

The hair slides farther into the punch. Three-quarters gone.

Chapter Eleven

$\mathcal{S}$OMEONE'S POUNDING THEIR FIST AGAINST MY CHEST. Bitch. Water rockets up through me, and I make sure to spurt it all into Petal's face.

I turn on my side and cough and splutter and choke the river water out onto the grass.

"Are you okay?" she asks.

My skin is wet. My clothes are wet. My throat is on fire. The wind whips through the sun-speckled grass and I *feel it.*

I'm alive.

The rush, the high from before I passed out, still lingers in my body. It will take a long time to go, fade out slowly, evaporate with the water that drips from my clothes.

And I got a memory back, too. I can feel myself smiling, my wet skin stretching as far as it can go.

I got a memory back. And finally, it's about us. Me, Mark, Pet, Amy.

Truth: I was not, am not, the good friend I'm pretending to be in my head.

My heart is still hammering in my rib cage. Erratic, wild, rock 'n' roll drumbeat. I'm horribly conscious of how loud my breathing is.

And oh, my god, I'm crazy, because I can almost see the gnome nodding along with me.

I hug the gnome to my chest. Cry for Amy. Silent tears that no one sees, because my face is wet and a few more drops of salt water don't really make a difference.

"Let's get out of here," Mark says, his voice firm, decisive.

Petal pulls me to my feet. Mark's already walking off, loping through the weeds with the rangy grace of a mountain lion. I'm about to follow him when Explosive Boy says, "Wait." He runs after Mark, grabs him, spins him around.

"Where the fuck do you think you're going?"

Mark raises his eyebrows. "Away from you."

Explosive Boy laughs, shakes his head. God. I swear I can see steam rolling from the ends of his hair. "No way," he says. "No way are you walking away from me after you pushed me off a fucking bridge. No way."

E's whole body is trembling. He always looks as if he's about to turn into a bonfire, but this is the first time I've really seen him ablaze. His fists curl and uncurl.

Mark notices and gives him a mocking smile. He does a few uppercuts and hops from foot to foot. "I may be a hippie, but I like my boxing classes, too."

Bullshit. Absolute bullshit. Whatever Mark knows about boxing he learned from watching the initial scenes of *Billy Elliot*. And even then, the ballet's more his forte.

Explosive Boy seems to have called Mark's bluff, because he takes a step toward him. Mark steps back, but he doesn't look worried. "Come on, E," Mark says. "You can't seriously have thought Pick Me Ups were going to be a tea party."

"You," E says, stepping through a clump of weeds, "are a dickhead."

Mark says something in reply, but I don't hear him because I'm still caught in the moment where E stepped through the weeds.

Amy died in a patch of weeds.

Suddenly, all my brain can think is that Amy's face is under E's foot. Her soft lips kissing the damp earth. I feel the ground on my own lips, my own face. Dirt, leaves, and a rubber sole pressing against my skin. Sealing off my mouth.

I hate my imagination.

My breaths sputter all over the place. Petal puts a hand on my back. "Okay," she says. "You're okay."

"Don't have a panic attack on us now, Ella," Mark says.

And when he turns to look at me, to make sure I'm all right, Explosive Boy arcs his fist through the air. There's no time for Mark to dodge out of the way. *Crunch*. E's knuckles find Mark's left cheekbone, and I can't help myself any longer, can't keep pretending to be okay when I can almost taste the dirt inside my mouth. I lean forward and hurl. Salt water and this morning's toast hit the ground.

Acid burns in my throat. Tears burn at the backs of my eyes.

I keep my head down. Let it knock against my knees. But I can still hear Mark yelling at Explosive Boy. "You little shit. I can't believe you actually hit me! Look what you've done to Ella."

"Me? You don't think it could have anything to do with the fact that you pushed me off a fucking bridge, and she had to jump in after me? You're the one who nearly drowned both of us."

My knees tremble, fold like soggy cardboard. I wind up kneeling in the dirt, desperately hoping that this doesn't turn into a panic attack. I vomit again. I just want to curl into a ball and shiver until my body warms up again.

But Petal wraps her arms around my waist, anchors me to the real world. "Don't you dare," she says, as if she somehow knows exactly what I'm thinking. "Don't you fucking dare, Ella Logan."

Her voice is so abrasive and bitchy and demanding. So familiar. It snaps me back into my body. And then she's whispering, "We're okay, we're okay, we're okay," like she needs to believe it's true.

My body trembles. Breaths gust in and out of me like gale force winds, blowing up my chest and then deflating it. "I'm okay," I wheeze. "I'm fine."

They all force smiles, but Explosive Boy can't even look at me. It's obvious that they don't believe what I've just said. Hard to do when vomit's decorating the ground in front of me. I take a step back, away from it. Close my eyes. God, I'm so disgusting.

"You asshole," Mark growls. I open my eyes because I don't think I've ever heard Mark this angry before. He's got a stripe on his left cheek where E hit him. It almost looks like war paint and matches the snarl threatening to rip his face apart.

There's a moment when I think hippie-pacifist Mark is actually going to hit someone—Mark may push people off bridges as a part of a Pick Me Ups initiation ritual; but actual violence, real violence, is something he hates.

In the end, though, he just sucks in a few deep breaths. Flashes his sideways smile. Goes back to being cool as a cucumber. I breathe a sigh of relief, because this is the probably smells terrible right now. "Don't you get it? I don't owe you anything. I don't know you; you don't know me."

And then he's the one attacking, moving way too close. He lets his head fall forward, and our foreheads meet. Breath kisses breath. "You owe me an orgy," he says. When he gives me my personal space back, he reaches into his jacket pocket, pulls out a box of Tic Tacs. Throws them at me.

I catch them, surprised. He gave me Kleenex, and I got him pushed off a bridge. Why the fuck would he give me anything after that?

He shrugs. "Your breath stinks, and I owe you. For saving my life. Consider us even now."

I reel because, shit, I saved his life. I saved this random boy's life, but I couldn't save my best friend's.

"Well," he's saying, "almost even. You still owe me that orgy."

Mark glowers at him. "I'm not participating."

"Did anyone ask you?"

Pet speaks up. "Let's just go home." Mark opens his mouth, doubtless to say that he doesn't want to go home, that he won't; but Petal glares at him. "All of us," she says firmly.

"Fine," Mark grumbles. I toss him his keys. He turns away and starts cutting through the bushes. "I'll see you

97

tomorrow," he calls over his shoulder. "We'll need to pay a visit to the barn."

Explosive Boy stares at me and Petal until she raises a single, slim eyebrow. "Didn't you hear?" she asks in a tone so bored it's insulting. "We'll see you tomorrow."

I watch, amused, as E reacts to Petal's disdain just like all the other kids at school—with a smile. A puppy dog smile that practically begs her to change her opinion of him, to like him. It's always this way with Petal. She likes nobody, wants nobody to like her; but everybody wants her to like them. No one is immune to her enigmatic charm, the combination of her looks and violent charisma. And she knows it, too.

Petal keeps her brow arched, tilts her head. She doesn't have to say anything more for Explosive Boy to know that he's been dismissed. He fades from sight, melting quickly into the trees.

Once he's gone, Petal grabs my arm and tries to tug me along, but I shake her away. "I can walk on my own."

She doesn't reply but stays beside me as we make our way through the trees. She stays beside me when we leave them, when we begin tramping down the leaf-littered streets of Sherwood. She stays beside me until we're standing outside of my house. God, I love her for that.

For a moment both of us stare at that spot on my front lawn, the one where Amy snapped her neck that night.

So when Explosive Boy taps on Cherry Bomb's window, I ignore him because he is neither past nostalgia nor future hope. Unfortunately, he pretends to ignore me ignoring him and keeps right on tapping away at the window.

"Ella," he says, his voice muffled by the glass. "Come on, open up."

Sigh. I twist myself out of my supine pose and open the door to make room for him on the backseat. He climbs in, bringing a stray leaf with him. It falls, an orange butterfly fluttering from the tattered corner of his blue jacket, to the car floor.

"Hi," he says.

I don't reply.

"So, where are we going today?"

I let out a deep breath and say, "Are you fucking serious—you want to come with us?"

Yesterday we pushed him off a bridge. Yesterday he punched Mark in the face. Yesterday I was certain that my plan to bring E into this strange game to spice things up had failed. That I had destroyed him appropriately, and he would never give me Kleenex or a pitiful look ever again.

Now I'm not sure.

"Yeah, I'm still interested in that orgy," he says in a tone that's so playful I know he's using it to mask something, to hide some other agenda.

And that's what stops me from telling him to get the hell out of the car. My curiosity about his hidden agenda. Well, that and my need to unite Mark and Pet and me. To make them spill the truth about the night Amy died.

"You'll see when you get there," I say to Explosive Boy.

He surprises me with his maple syrup smile. As if he doesn't give a fuck that I'm being a bitch to him. "Going to blindfold me again?" he asks.

"No." I check the time—ten minutes before the last class lets out. "But Mark will be here soon, and he may want you to get the fuck out of his car. No guarantees that you can actually come along for this ride."

"I'd better make the best of my time here, then," E says, nodding. He leans back, folding his arms behind his head. Then he kicks up his feet, draping them over the front seat. He drums his muddy feet against Cherry Bomb's already-ruined leather and gives me an angelic smile.

I snort. "Mature. Wasn't punching the guy enough?"

"Let's see," Explosive Boy says, squinting as if he's thinking real hard. "He pushed me off a bridge and nearly killed me. I punched him and messed up his car a little. We're *totally* even."

That shocks a laugh out of me. Yes, sarcasm is the lowest form of wit—but it's still a form of wit. I wasn't expecting much wit from E. Just endless brooding and gunpowder cologne.

"So you are pissed off about that?" I ask him.

His jaw tightens. "Pissed off is the tip of the fucking iceberg," he says. "But short of punching you, I'm not sure how to deal with that emotion. And I don't hit girls."

"You sexist pig."

He raises an eyebrow. "You're impossible to please, aren't you?"

"Basically."

He shakes his head and pulls an iPod from the pocket of his tatty jacket. "Want to listen?" he asks, holding out an earbud to me.

I take it because there's nothing else to do. But when I put it into my ear, when I hear the song he's listening to, I wish that I hadn't. "This was Amy's favorite song," I say, swallowing hard.

"Little Wing," Jimi Hendrix. She always said she could hear velvet in this music. Rich, purple velvet and sex.

"Your friend, right?" he says. "The one who died? I'm sorry."

I pick at the foam spilling from Cherry Bomb's ruptured upholstery. I can feel his eyes on me. In my peripheral vision, I watch his lips part. But before he can say anything else, the car door swings open.

Mark. Today's scarf is highlighter yellow, and he's got

a lollipop in his mouth again. He raises his eyebrows at E. "Comfortable?" he asks in a tone that implies he's once more on the brink of committing an act of lollipop violence.

E removes his feet from the front seat and slings an arm around me. "Oh," he says, shuffling slightly closer to me, bringing the smell of gunpowder with him, "very."

"Ha. Ha. Ha. Just hilarious," I say, putting the distance back between us, letting the smell of gunpowder fade away.

E drops his arm from my shoulder and smiles sheepishly. "Sorry," he says as Mark starts up Cherry Bomb's engine.

Mark ignores him. "Petal's meeting us there," he says.

We don't speak on the way to the barn, but E keeps "Little Wing" on repeat. And Jimi Hendrix croons and croons and croons in my ear about a girl with a circus mind and a thousand free smiles.

When we enter the barn, Petal waves to us from the third floor. Maybe watching me jump off a bridge has emboldened her.

I climb the stairs, ignoring the looks Mark and E give me. On the second floor, I turn back to them. "Coming?" I ask.

They follow, grumbling.

"This is not a good idea." Mark's lost the lollipop, but he hasn't yet managed to find a convincingly serious expression. I doubt that day will ever come.

"Well," I say, "as the inventor of Pick Me Ups, you, my dear Marcus, are not allowed to comment on what is and isn't a bad idea."

I reach the third floor ahead of Mark and E, and Petal immediately points to a space in the middle of the barn. I follow her finger. The gnome's glossy ceramic coat winks up at me from the bales of hay.

I smile to thank her for bringing my ref as Mark and E join us.

Mark takes a look over the edge, and his face pales. It's a long way to fall. He steps back from the edge and starts yammering about plans to get a gun so we can play Russian roulette instead. Pet bobs her head up and down like a buoy in the ocean. But we all know there's nothing about this buoy that's going to keep her afloat.

I am silent, but unafraid. Completely unafraid. I slide toward the edge. Creep toward my fall.

E puts a hand on my shoulder before I can get too far. "Why?" he asks. "Why do you do this?"

I don't say anything, and neither does Mark. But Petal—softhearted Petal—finally gives E the explanation he's been hankering after. About Pick Me Ups. About Amy. And even as she says it all, even as she tells him about how Mark thought we could use Pick Me Ups to understand Amy, it sounds forced and stupid. Because it's more than that. It's so much fucking more than that.

Explosive Boy doesn't seem too convinced. "Is this really the best way for you guys to get close to Amy?" he asks. "And I mean, no offense, but I didn't even know Amy. There's really not much of a reason for me to be tossing myself off shit and putting a gun to my head. I don't want to die."

He doesn't get it. Pick Me Ups aren't only about death. They're about really, truly feeling the world around you. They're about the rush. The way the blood floods your head, pounds in your eardrums. The wind whistling by as you fall. And of course, the adrenaline spike when you hit the ground.

This is about living as much as it is about dying. About pleasure as much as it is about pain.

Petal shakes her head at E. "You don't understand anything," she says, echoing my thoughts. "What are you even doing here? You just want to get into Ella's pants, don't you?" She raises her eyebrows. If he says no, she'll make social mincemeat of him at school.

We know. He knows.

But judging by the grin on his face, he doesn't care. Maybe Explosive Boys don't do well socially, anyway.

"You got me." He holds up his hands, palms out.

Surrenders. "But jumping off things isn't going to get me into Ella's pants. And almost killing yourself isn't going to get you into Amy's mind."

"What do you know? *What?*" My voice shrieks, grating like sandpaper against his cheeks. I can practically see it obliterating his freckles. I want to swear so fucking badly. But swearing would be an admission that he's right.

He isn't. Pick Me Ups are worth it. I'm getting my memories back.

"I know a lot about coming to terms with grief," E answers.

Petal's arm is raised, fingers curling toward the palm. Half fist. It quivers as if it's not an extension of her body but something separate. Something with a mind of its own. Floundering, hovering above the hay.

Ready to strike.

E grins at her. "And you look like such a pretty girl—"

I punch E on the shoulder. Not too hard, but hard enough for him to know that if he says that again we'll lob him straight into the bales of hay below. And this time I won't leap after him, won't make sure he's okay.

Petal's lying to me, sure; but, hell, she's still my friend. No one messes with my friends. *No one messes with us.* Amy used to make sure of it when she was alive. It feels like my job now, for some reason. Maybe because Amy, as much as she linked us together, was the odd one out.

Amy was the one who felt isolated the most—and she didn't shut up about it, either. If there was one thing Amy wasn't insecure about, it was her insecurity. And in some ways that made her a stronger person than I'll ever be.

Outwardly, I don't whine.

Outwardly, sticks and stones don't break my bones.

Inwardly, I'm worse than Holden Caulfield.

I try to shake myself out of my thoughts and into the real world, but it's like there's a barrier between my body and my soul and the air. Detached, I'm so detached.

And I look at the hay, and I can't help but think of straw floating up around me like a lazily blown kiss. The rush of the wind and the roar of my memories. I want to walk down this road. I want to retrieve another piece of my memory.

So I walk. I walk to the edge, and I meet the merry, beetle-black eyes of the gnome.

It's high time one of us tried the third floor.

Only E's face makes me pause. Horrified wrinkles have knitted themselves into the edges of his mouth where the laugh lines should be. Fingers, tangled and knotted through bonfire hair. He transforms into an exaggerated version of *The Scream*, roaring colors rushing by behind him. "Don't—"

And the moment he says it, I do.

The air slides away beneath my feet.

And the greater the height, the greater the rush—it works.

Memories roar up to catch me. I bounce into their bittersweet embrace.

"Ella, Ella, Ella."

She's drunk. Amy's wasted, and I'm beginning to wonder whether that brownie she ate was really all brownie. Because she's acting so fucking weird.

Under the table, Mark has Amy's hand clasped in his. He's singing a soft lullaby to her: "Hush little baby, don't you cry . . ."

But Amy's not a little kid anymore, and she's not having any of it. She leaves her hand in Mark's but lets the silence sit between them, lets it burn away the air in the room until we're all suffocating.

We're still playing the game, still asking the questions in a circle, and it's Amy's turn. Amy's turn again.

She laughs and laughs and laughs for no reason. Then she turns straight to me and says, "Ella. When you said you wanted out last week in PE, what did you mean? I never bothered to ask you." She knocks her head into her palms. "I should have asked you. I mean, you could have just meant you wanted out of PE—but, oh, god, I'm such a bad friend."

I wonder, How does she know?

I trace circles on the tabletop. No one should be able to get this close to me. I want to tell them all to fuck off, to get lost, because sometimes I say things and I don't want my meaning to be demanded. But Amy's looking at me with those eyes of hers, drunk. Red spider lines from the alcohol. An eyelash drifting like snow onto her cheek. She regards me seriously, because, yeah, she's drunk. But she still loves me.

Alcohol can't take away love.

And I love her back.

It wouldn't hurt to say this now, would it? They're too tipsy to remember anything.

Fine. I'll tell them the truth.

"I— No, I didn't mean that I wanted out of PE. I meant"—I wave my hands around—"I meant I wanted out of it all. Everything, you know. The chaos. I just . . . I wanted a bit of peace and quiet. Silence."

As I say the words, something breaks away in my chest. My feelings have found a place to rest. Atlas shrugs. The world falls off my shoulders into a bowl of punch.

And Amy, eyes wide, brighter than the stars, she stares at me. The doof-doof-doof *beat of the psychedelic music blares through her pause, filling up the silence. "You mean, like,* suicide?"

Facedown in the straw. Did I pass out? My name is ringing in my ears.

E, Mark, Pet. Faces floating above me, islands of cloud.

"Ella, unless you sit up in the next ten seconds, E's going to pull a Prince Charming and kiss you out of your sleep."

"She—" I begin. "I—it was my fault."

My limbs feel as if someone's poured tar over them.

They refuse to move at the speed of my thoughts. I sludge my way into an upright position.

Mark grins. "I see my threat worked."

"I'm not that bad a kisser, you know."

"Shut up," I choke. I remember. I've just remembered. "It wasn't Amy. It wasn't— It was me. I put the idea into her head."

The words flop from my mouth and circle around my neck. A noose made of vocabulary, thought, memory.

The neck of my soul snaps.

Just like Amy's.

Because, shit, is it really all my fault?

"What do you mean, it was your idea?" Petal asks.

"I wanted to commit suicide first," I say. "It was me and my stupid big mouth."

Fuck the stupid spiked punch. Fuck it for unhinging my mouth so that it swung wide-open, allowing Amy to see into my soul. For allowing Amy to see herself reflected in me.

But I'd thought they'd be too drunk to remember what I'd said.

"What?" Mark says, his head swinging from side to side. "No-o-o," he says slowly, as if trying to drive a stake through my mind with that word.

"What do you mean, no?" My breath blows hay out of my hair. Did my words blow Amy off my rooftop?

"He means, Ella, that you wanting to die was kind of old news." Petal's fingers, decorated with metal rings, slip beneath my shoulders, and she picks me up. Hauls me to my feet, for the second time this week.

"We knew," she says. "Even though you never said it." Pause. She looks at Mark. "Right?"

His eyes are focused on the hay; and when he looks up, he's got this ridiculously big smile pasted on his face.

Mark has an inability to be serious for longer than ten seconds. It makes him awkward-awkward-awkward in situations like this. He sighs, shrugs. All with the ridiculous smile in place. Then he opens his mouth.

For a second I think he's going to say "Wheee!" but he doesn't. Guess even Mark knows that some moments are beyond childhood, beyond the Peter Pan games he likes to play with himself.

"Yeah, I knew," he says. "I knew about you before you said it, Ella. And Amy, too. I figured it was why you guys were always so close, you know?"

I do.

Even though I loved Mark and Pet with all my heart, it was always Amy who could get me to do anything.

One word from Amy, and I'd be up at five in the morning to get a coffee, have a picnic, fuck up some kid's morning with barbed-wire words.

I can't believe I'm only realizing this now. Amy always

claimed that she was on the outside, and I thought so, too. But she wasn't. We were together, the two of us.

I stare at him. At Petal. How can you just *know* something like that? I mean, yeah, we're good friends; but this goes beyond friendship. This is like psychic ability. It's creepy, in the same way it would be creepy if a ten-year-old told you he understood everything about calculus.

"It's kind of obvious, though," E murmurs softly. "With you, Ella. I mean, it was the first thing I thought when I saw you." He's standing off to the side, slants of shadow filtering into the barn with the sunshine, obscuring his features.

"What, exactly, did you think?"

"I thought," he says, "I thought—"And he comes closer and closer until his shoulder knocks against mine and I can hear the rasp of his breaths, feel their warmth.

A bullet of a boy is whispering in my ear. And what he's saying is far from sweet nothings. "I thought your eyes were dead. I thought, 'How long can she keep up this way?'"

Chapter Thirteen

E BREAKS OUR SILENCE TO ASK ME THAT SAME DAMN QUES-
tion as we walk to the child care center. "Seriously, Ella,
how long can you last like this?"

I tell him what I tell myself after each fall. What I tell
myself when the pain has faded to a dull ache, a drumbeat
that *thud*, *thud*, *thud*s through my body. "Forever, probably.
It's not too bad."

He eyes my bloodied knee and bruised left arm, and
I get it; I do. My body is telling him a different story. My
body is saying that it cannot do this forever because this is
fucking unhealthy. But so is chocolate, and I'm not giving
that up any time soon.

"Cut it out, okay, E? You just look like you're perving
on me."

"What did you think I was doing?" he asks, winking;
but he looks away immediately, and his concern is so freaking obvious, it slays me.

I feel the need to say something, so I go with, "I'm fine."

He laughs at me and pulls out his iPod again. "If you're just going to lie to me . . ." He makes to put his earbuds on, but I stop him by playfully punching him on the arm.

"Okay," I say, "I'll revise that to I *will* be fine. Better?"

He puts his iPod away but says nothing. Just examines me with heavy, lidded eyes as if he doesn't know whether to believe me or not. And I run my hand down my rib cage, my battered rib cage, and look away. Because I don't know whether or not to believe me, either.

I thought I'd killed E's annoying concern on the walk over here, but it rears its monstrous head again once we've finished signing in at the child care center. "Look," he says. "I can handle everything today. You just avoid the screaming children and go sit down, okay?"

He's not getting rid of me that easily. No way am I accepting more pity from Explosive Boy. "Oh, but screaming children are my favorite." I follow him to where the children are standing, ignoring the pain that shoots through my legs and E's irritated expression.

"I told you to sit down," he says to me quietly.

"And I said I like screaming children."

"Well, do you like to be the reason *why* they're screaming?"

Oh. Point taken. My skin is a tangle of bruises and blood.

Explosive Boy reaches out and smooths a hand over my hair, tucks some of it behind my ears. His fingers ghost dangerously close to my skin. "You look like crap right now," he says.

"Don't you just know how to make a girl feel special?"

"It's a family talent." He flashes me his maple syrup smile. "Seriously, though. Sit down before they freak out. They're already staring at you."

And so they are. Beady children's eyes cling to every part of my body, taking in my bloodied knees and torn T-shirt. My bruised arms and the cuts crosshatched over my hands.

"Right," I say. "Probably for the best."

I make my way to the green bench in the corner of the yard. The same one I sat on last time I was here, before Casey called me out to play duck, duck, goose with the others. The building casts a long shadow over half of it, and I make sure to fold myself into that darkness, hoping that no one will see me. Hoping that no one will hear the tightness of my breathing.

It's a hollow hope.

E follows me over to the bench as soon as the kids are settled.

"Are you okay?" he asks.

I can't help but laugh. I'm the one who helped him get pushed off a bridge just yesterday.

"Are *you*? After what we did—"

His expression changes immediately.

The silence is a loaded gun. Its barrel swings back and forth, back and forth, between E and I. Finally, he says, "I'm A-OK. Crazy people push me off bridges every fucking day. No sweat, really."

The anger in his voice wraps itself around the gun. Lock and load, baby. Pull the trigger.

Boom.

The silence blows my head right off.

Pieces of my mind skid across the concrete. I try to piece them back together again, but it's hard with Explosive Boy roasting me alive with his stare.

"Are you ever going to apologize?" he asks me.

My mind's only half recollected, but still words wobble out my mouth. "For what? For saving your life?"

He shakes his head, sprays of red hair torching the air around him, and laughs. "You just don't get it," he says, and then he's walking back to the children; and god, I'm just relieved that he doesn't pity me anymore.

For a minute I enjoy nothing but silence, pain, and a dirty stare from Heather when she pops out to check on things. But then Casey crawls onto the bench.

"Hi," she says.

"Hey."

I resist the urge to bury my head in my hands.

She looks me and up and down. "What happened to you?"

"I fell down," I say truthfully.

"Are you all right?" She's found a twig and is busy clacking it against the bench over and over and over again.

"Yeah, I'm fine," I say. She doesn't reply, just keeps on going with that goddamn twig; and it's giving me a headache, so I snap, "Do you have a career as a drummer in mind or what?"

She stops playing with the twig and looks at me with those big, brown eyes of hers. "Nope," she says. "Wanna know what I'd actually like to be?" She uses the twig to scrape some of the peeling green paint off the bench. The paint flakes into a million pieces, and she blows it off the bench like other little girls blow away dandelion seeds.

"Sure," I say. Pain stabs through my knee, and I cover it with my hand. Sharp sting. I savor the pain but will it to go away at the same time.

"I want to be a mechanic," Casey says, smiling.

I nod. Once, twice, three times. "I can see that," I say. "Will you wear a jumpsuit and have oil stains all over you?"

Casey shakes her head madly and kicks her legs against the bench. "No way! I'd like to change things up a bit, you know?" She twists her lips to the side, an expression of intense concentration. "I'd like to be a mechanic who wears a lace dress, maybe. Yeah. A white lace dress."

She lifts her head, and so do I. We watch the sky together.

I open my mouth, about to tell her how ridiculous that sounds, but then I remember what my own dream was when I was ten years old: to become an anthropologist who studied the nightlife in Sherwood. Because Sherwood is just teeming with nightlife.

So I allow for her subversive child's dream. "Sounds good."

And as soon as I say it, give her that green light, she's off. Telling me about her million-and-one other plans. She sounds hungry. Hungry for someone to listen, hungry for someone to tell her that her dreams are not simply castles in the air and can come true. She likes science and music, Casey. She wants to understand the world and then write songs expressing its beauty.

All while fixing cars in a white lace dress.

When the center's about to close, when all the other kids have left and E is walking over to us, Casey asks, "Do you really think I can do it?" Her voice cracks down the middle in doubt.

"Of course."

"It's just that my mom says—"

119

E reaches us before she finishes her sentence, but I can guess its ending. Casey looks at her shoelaces, bites her lip. She smiles at E and me. "Bye," she says, and then she's gone, before I can tell her that dreams, anyone's dreams—however small or big or outlandish—are worth a damn. No matter what anyone's mother says.

Chapter Fourteen

THE NEXT MORNING I BUMP INTO MY MOTHER IN THE kitchen.

We both move awkwardly from side to side trying to avoid the other. Eventually, I give up and stand stock-still, not allowing her to get past me.

"Shouldn't you be at work?"

She's dressed for it. Clean, crisp blue business suit with a pair of sheer stockings. But then this is my mother's usual ensemble. I haven't seen her wearing anything else in the past few years.

Sometimes I think she sleeps in her suits.

"My meeting got canceled," she says. "Shouldn't you be at school?" Her voice is knife-sharp.

"I'm running a little late," I say.

And suddenly, I'm aware of my morning breath, the stink that hangs about my words. My brittle, breaking hair. The fact that I'm clad in a fucking pink nightie with a suggestive comment about how good I am in bed scrawled across it.

There isn't a hair out of place on my mother's head.

I'm not exactly sure what my mother does. She's never explained it properly because it's apparently beyond my comprehension—all I know is that it's some corporate shit in a bank. She probably spends her days shredding paper and stealing souls while looking the epitome of neat and tidy.

She pats down her already perfectly smooth hair. "Honey." The word tastes sweet, too sweet. "I'll give you a ride to school," she says, just as the phone rings. She stalks into the living room, and I follow her, watching as she lifts the receiver to her ear.

"Amanda Logan speaking," she says. "Oh, Jillian, how lovely to hear from you. You're in the Bahamas, aren't you?"

There's a pause as Jillian, who is a complete stranger to me, says something.

Mom replies, "Yes, in our front garden," and I know, instantly, that they're talking about Amy. "It was a tragedy." Jillian says something else, something that makes my mother glare at me. "No, we didn't give her the alcohol—Michael and I were in DC when she threw the party," she says, waving a hand as if to dismiss the entire thing, even though Jillian can't see her. She's lying, too. I don't know where Dad was, but he wasn't in DC with Mom. "You know how these things go. She's a brilliant girl, so talented; she's just made a few youthful indiscretions."

I lift my eyes to the ceiling. For the entire first week after Amy died, my mother had to defend me to people like this. Jillian must have missed the memo on my bad behavior because of her Bahamas trip. "That's okay about the ride, Mom," I say, calling her away from Jillian for a second. "Mark will probably swing by soon."

Mark always swings by. He has ever since he got his license. But after Amy died, he only gives me lifts to school on certain days. Other days we go to the mall, Ghost Town, the local pool.

Once or twice we've gone to the barn.

"Listen, Jill. I'm so sorry, but I have to go. I've got something on the stove and it's burning, but I look forward to seeing you when you get home!" She clicks the cordless phone back into its cradle and turns to me.

"You're not waiting for Mark." She glares at me for what seems like the millionth time this morning, as if she knows exactly what we've been up to. Her lips tighten into a toothpick-thin line. "I'm driving you to school." She readjusts her suit, picks up her car keys.

Guess this business meeting's over.

• • •

In the car, she insists on talking to me.

MOM: So how was the child care center yesterday?

ME: Sadistic.

MOM: Ella, I know it's hard for you to see this right now, but I'm just trying to help. I'm not trying to be sadistic.

ME: I didn't mean you. I meant that everyone there is a sadist, especially my boss. And the children are perverts.

MOM: I'm sure it's not that bad.

ME: They're either drawing some seriously fucked-up bananas or penises on that blackboard, Mom.

MOM: Watch your mouth.

Cue silence. It hums and thrums between us.

Eventually, Mom departs from her usually perfect driving behavior: she takes her eyes off the road and trains them on me. They linger on my scabby knee.

Mom's lip curls. This is not a face of concern. This is a face of Contempt and Shame.

She pulls into the school parking lot and reverse-parks expertly, settling the car securely between the white lines. She even manages to avoid the pothole at the back of this car space.

I swear, sometimes it's as if my mother's inhuman.

She stares straight ahead, through the windshield at

the boring brick wall of my school, and swallows. "Ella," she says.

Is it possible that I scare this woman?

"Ella, are you—"

"I have to go or I'll be late."

I open the door, kick my legs out of the car and onto the pavement. I turn back to my mother, a good-bye ready on my lips. But she's opening her mouth again, and I'm sure something hideous is about to crawl out.

I slam the door shut before I can hear what it is. Her words pummel the window instead of me.

Meeting. Fucking. Adjourned.

But I know what she was going to say. *I know.* Her words stalk me across the parking lot. They ring in my ears, loud and clear.

I'm sorry, honey, so sorry; but this situation really is of your own making. . . .

She's said it before. She keeps on saying it. Every time she bothers to talk to me. Which is usually whenever I look too sad. Whenever I stop being fine, fine, fine.

It kills me, because I know she's right. Despite what the school counselor told me in that one session we had right after Amy died. *It's not your fault. You should never think it's your fault.*

But who threw the party?

Who let wine and whiskey and beer and vodka-spiked punch into the place?

Who drank so much that she can't remember shit about the party?

Me. Me. Me, again.

I'm a fucked-up daughter because I threw the stupid, stereotypical, suburban-idiot party. I'm a fucked-up friend because I didn't look out for Amy.

Where the fuck was I when she fell?

What happened that night? It's a question that's always on my mind. It's a question that I'm willing to sacrifice anything to finally answer.

Because I don't think I can live with myself if I don't know.

Still, I wish Mom wouldn't constantly remind me of my failure. It's not as if I tell her every time I see her that the situation with Dad is *all of your own making, honey.*

And that's true, too.

Chapter Fifteen

THURSDAY PASSES LIKE ANY OTHER SCHOOL DAY: SLOWLY. I attend half my classes and spend the other half sitting next to Amy's old locker, fiddling with the combination lock. They've reset her password and given it to some other student already. A girl named Justine. I heard one of her friends calling to her this morning when she was standing beside Amy's locker. Watched the swish of her blond hair as she turned to answer with a smile.

She seemed totally unaware that her locker used to belong to someone else. That her locker used to belong to the dead girl.

After school I make one last visit to that corridor. I take in the dust motes floating in the colorful light streaming through the stained glass windows—the space already feels somehow different. Somehow lesser.

And it's a fear, a fear that makes itself heard above the constant ache from my bruises. The world will move on. The world will move on without Amy, and I'll be left there standing still in a river of time. My hands splashing desperately through the waters around me, trying to catch the truth, trying to catch something, and always finding nothing.

I avoid Mark and Petal in the parking lot. Don't even dare to look over at Cherry Bomb as I walk on by. Because my body may crave a Pick Me Up. But today my mind is too wrecked to play their games. To deal with Mark's sideways smile, Petal's extended silences.

I go straight home instead.

I go straight home; and in my bedroom, with so many useless, desperate thoughts to avoid and nothing better to distract me from them, I devour my homework as if it's a Family fucking Feast.

I speed through my calc questions, English notes on Act 1 of *Hamlet*, science and history. When it's all gone, when the notes for each subject are taken and lying in piles on my desk with colorful, annotated tabs sticking out the sides, I'm winded.

As if I've run a marathon.

I choke and wheeze among piles of homework. Because when there's nothing else, no homework to distract me, no lying friends to puzzle the truth out of, I feel myself starting to lose it.

My fingers are shaking. My hands are shaking. I clamp

down on the desk to try and stop the tremors passing through me, but that doesn't work. The table just rattles along with me. Fuck. This. Shit.

Anxiety attacks are, apparently, normal when you don't like the fact that your best friend threw herself off your roof. And landed in front of your garden gnome.

I get up, take a few deep breaths. It feels as if I'm running over jelly instead of carpet when I cross the room, open the door, and zip through the hall. Slide out the front door.

Run and run and run and run. I'm still barefoot. Grass slips between my toes. Sun-warmed pavement smashes into my blisters, burning me. I wince but keep running, and the ground starts to fall away beneath me. Starts to feel slippery like jelly, all too easy to sink into.

I've had panic attacks before—before Amy died, that is. I used to have them on game days for basketball, when I was all keyed up and so terrified of passing the ball to the wrong person.

That's why I gave up basketball. Because I was scared of making mistakes.

I wonder whether I gave up on Amy for the same reason. Because I was afraid I'd screw up things.

I keep blaming it on myself. And I know I shouldn't,

because it's whiny and because the school counselor's a professional, an expert; and she told me that it wasn't, wasn't, wasn't my fault.

But what if it is?

I brought it up. I almost suggested it to Amy, didn't I?

But maybe it was like Mark and Pet said before, how you can tell stuff about a person sometimes. Apparently, I'm an open book full of blank pages, but even E can read my cover.

How long can she keep up this way? he wondered.

"Forever," I wheeze. "Forever," I spit defiantly at the brilliant blue sky, at the pavement, at the grass that I step onto. It tickles my feet as if greeting my defiance with laughter.

And the grass is right to laugh because, crap, I'm not a machine. My panting breaths hit the grass; my hands hit my knees.

On the upside, when blood roars through my head like this, when my breath comes in short, sharp gasps, the world solidifies. The sensation of running through jelly and sinking into quicksand disappears.

I'm in someone else's yard, and I reach out and wrap my arm around a low-hanging tree branch to steady myself. And before I know what I'm doing, I'm swinging my legs up, too. Arms circling the branch, feet crossed over the wood. My body hangs, suspended. Wind rushes through the crevice between my stomach, my knees, and the branch.

Blood rushes to my head because of the almost upside-down position I'm in.

I swing, swing, swing myself upright.

My teeth chatter as I stretch out my hands to catch the next branch. I'm swinging again, twisting myself up and over. In eighth-grade gym class, my teachers said I showed some promise on the bars—flips, back rolls, hanging positions, they were all easy for me—but I was never this good.

Even last year my arms would have given out.

But after Amy died? God, the number of times I've climbed the tree outside my bedroom window. The number of times I've sat on my roof at midnight and thought about smashing into the weeds in my garden—not dying, but smashing into the weeds.

The sun is falling around me, and it feels as if the sky is melting into the tree. I feel my feet against the branches, feel how easy it would be to slip and fall.

Splat. In the grass.

But the gnome isn't here, and there are no weeds to lose myself in.

So I just haul myself up onto the next branch and let my legs dangle above the ground. The thin branch bends, and there's this moment when I'm thinking, *Snap, come on, snap.*

But then I see someone jogging down the road, cutting through the melting sunset. It's E. And when he sees me—and the bending branch—he breaks into a run. A run so fast he goes from grenade to bullet.

I have no idea why he insists on giving a shit about me, and I have no idea what he thinks running's going to do. I'm up a tree; it's climbing skills he needs right now.

As he nears the tree, it becomes clear that he's barreling along so fast he's not going to be able to stop.

Wham! Bark crashes down around him. He topples back onto the prickly carpet of grass. *"Oof,"* he says.

Maybe I should flip him off. Or I could tell him to go away and never come back. But I decide to play things cool. I kick my legs through the chilly evening air. "How you doing, E?"

He glares up at me. "It's *Tristan*, Ella," he says. "I know you want to get with me, but turning our names into some screwed-up alliteration isn't going to do the trick."

I raise my eyebrows and pull a Mark. "Coooooeeeeee!" I call into the fading light. Then I start singing "Humpty Dumpty" really loudly because I know it'll piss him off. I can see him connecting the dots in his mind. Ella's sitting on a wall. Ella could fall off the wall, and would all the king's horses and all the king's men be able to put her together again?

But Ella's a bitch. And Humpty was just a nice egg of

a guy, so we really can't draw any parallels between the two stories, can we?

I wait for him to interrupt me, but he doesn't. When I glance at him he's totally silent, rays of sunlight dying behind his head, setting him on fire.

I sing louder. So loud that someone opens their window to yell "Shut up!" at me.

I'm not sure where the voice came from, so I give the finger to every house on the street. The lacy curtains in one house drop back into position quickly. Trust the owners of lacy fucking curtains to be spoilsports.

Amy's parents owned—own—lacy curtains.

In the process of laughing and making sure my finger is pointing straight at the curtain owners, I slip. My adrenaline spikes, flies away into the twilight as I begin to fall. But I manage to grab the branch just in time.

E's shouting up at me, "Ella, come on. Come down. This won't solve anything."

"What won't?" I ask him, dangling.

"Jumping like Amy."

"Fuck off. I wasn't intending to do that."

"Okay, so that's why you should come down."

Bullets cannot be gentle. Grenades cannot be gentle. He's still holding back.

"Relax, I'm not going to kill myself. I just wanted to see the pretty scenery."

"So come down for fuck's sake."

And there it is. An explosive voice, for my Explosive Boy. "Okay, I'll jump down—"

"That's not what I meant!"

"But it's how I want to get down. Are you forgetting what Pick Me Ups are? What we're doing to always remember Amy?"

"But you're not trying to remember Amy, are you?" He's shouting, hands tangling through his hair.

The lacy-curtain owner yells something about the police at us. I'm surprised to see he's a big man with a beer belly. Normally the threat of police, of authority would make me budge. But I feel about as dead inside as the twigs spattered over the ground.

So I yell, "Oh, go fuck yourself!"

At the same time as E yells, "The cops can fuck themselves!"

We both burst out laughing. Lacy-curtain-beer-gut shoves his window shut.

"Good riddance," I mutter.

"Come down, Ella." E's voice is softer now.

"What do you mean I don't want to remember Amy? And I don't even know you. Why do you care about me? Why don't you just, sort of, go away?"

"Go away?" His laugh slices through the air. "Okay, number one, you were a part of a plan to shove me off a bridge. And then you saved my life. Whether or not you like it, you know me. We're fucking *acquaintances* at the very least. I care about you because I'd care about anyone who was sitting in a tree like an idiot. And I can't go away because I'd feel guilty forever if I kept walking to the supermarket and left you here."

Oh, thank god. The knots in my stomach untie themselves. He didn't come here looking for me; he's just going shopping.

I realize he's waiting for a response. So I shrug, because it seems like a safe thing to do. No one can like you, hate you, feel anything about you if you go through life shrugging.

He fixes me with this look. This look that tells me he knows I'm playing with him and he'd really appreciate it if I dropped the act.

I shrug my shoulders again. To piss him off, yeah. But also because really, this is who I am. I am all act with nothing underneath. I have constructed myself like an IKEA kitchen. Sturdy on the outside but hollow and unstable on the inside.

I really only have one mode, one attitude. Maybe that's why it pisses me off when Explosive Boy goes from gunpowder and smoke to Kid Whisperer to fucking chivalry, like it's the easiest thing in the world. Like he doesn't feel he has to be a certain way all the time.

"Can I ask you a question?" E asks, cutting through my thoughts.

"Just did. And I'm answering: no."

He ignores me and continues. "Can you just be nice for one goddamn second?"

"Another question. But sure I can." I make my voice sweet, sugary. "How can I help you, sir?"

He shudders. "Not that nice. That's just scary—what I'm saying is, be a normal person and get out of the freaking tree, okay, Ella?"

"But I'm not normal."

"Pretend. You know you're good at it."

What the fuck is that supposed to mean?

I don't want to hear the answer, so I don't ask.

Instead, I act as if I'm thinking about his proposition seriously. I even scratch my chin and toy with an imaginary beard. "Well," I say eventually, drawing out the word, "what's in it for me?"

"If you come down," he says, "I promise to help you find out how Amy *really* felt before she died."

Leaves whisper against my skin, and I turn my face to catch the sunlight, only to find it gone. Darkness curls around me. "No one could possibly know how she felt."

My voice is so low that I'm surprised he catches the words.

"No, that's true. No one could ever fully understand. But I've been to that place with someone else before. My brother. He was suffering all his life, Ella. Everything—" Fiery sobs in the still night air. Explosive Boy is not meant to do this. He's not meant to implode like this.

It hits me then that yeah, I'm messed up; but this guy's got some problems, too. Should've guessed based on the fact that he smells like gunpowder and skips class in the middle of storms to take mud baths out on the football field.

"Right," I say. "Right."

Somehow my weak voice gives him the courage to go on. He swallows the fire. But now that I know it's there, I can see it, burning through the blood that pumps under his skin. Struggling to get out.

"Everything went wrong for Ethan." He meets my eyes now. "I used to call him E—"

Guilt trips me, makes me want to fall off the branch onto the grass below. If some dipshit started calling me Ames every ten seconds, I'd probably strangle them.

So E's going to be Tristan from now on. "Shit. Sorry. You should have said something."

And I still sound like a bitch. My cold, unfeeling, metallic voice makes the night air tangy. Rusty.

Tristan takes it like a man. Doesn't bat an eyelid, an eyelash. "Ethan took pills when he turned sixteen. I was fourteen then. My brother died in my bedroom." And suddenly he's gone—not literally, but I can see him running in his mind. Avoiding the memory.

Eyes glazed over. Lips trembling. "He vomited a lot at the end—"

I'm reminded of myself in the park, of the vomit that Tristan could barely look at. Things are snapping into place now, the way a broken bone does when a doctor sets it. "Right."

My vocabulary is obviously limited to *right* and *fuck* at the moment.

"My sheets were all messed up."

His *sheets*? Yeah. Like that's the most important thing that got messed up. Reading between the lines, I'd say Tristan wants me to replace *my sheets* with *my life, my mind, my world*. Because when someone you love does that to themselves, everything in the universe starts to spin like a top.

And you get so dizzy that you know the world's going to topple and so are you.

"Come down, Ella."

And in the deepening night, I make my way back down. It's not as smooth a process as it was going up. Rough bark scratches my skin. Two of my nails break.

I reach the ground and stand next to Tristan. Our breaths rise in puffs, clouds that intertwine in the evening air. We face the lacy white curtains, and I point at them and say, "What a dick, right?" so that we don't have to talk about *why* I was up a tree or his brother anymore.

He laughs, and it's at that moment that we hear the rumble of an engine. I look at Tristan, look up at the tree, look at the long road ahead. Shit, there's a police car at the top of it.

"Run?" he asks. As if running away from cops is a decision that needs to be made in a democratic way.

"Hell, yes!" I reply. But then I just stand there, shocked that for the first time ever someone really did call the cops on me.

It doesn't matter that my insides feel like molasses because the car is moving slowly, like the cop knows it's Mr. Lacy Curtains who's narced on us and he doesn't have to worry.

But Tristan, *he's* looking worried. His eyebrows stitch themselves together, and he seizes my hand and starts to run. "Come on, Ella. Come on."

As we pick up speed, I shake him off. Run on my own. Because on my own is how I do things. But as finger after warm finger slips off my hand, I remember letting go of another hand in another place and time.

Two wrists in the moonlight.

"Starlight, star bright," says Mark. "Starliiiiight."

He's watching us. Me and Amy, standing there with our fingers curled through each other's. We're in my garden. In my peripheral vision, I can see the gnome.

"Are you in, Ella?" Amy says.

Doof, doof, doof. *The beat of the music makes it easy, so easy for a head to bob up and down in a nod. But I shake off the music, shake my head. "I don't think it's a good idea."*

Her hand slides from mine. Finger after finger after finger. And then suddenly my hand is free, all of her warmth and weight gone. My fingers trail through the cool inkwell of evening, feeling discon- nected. How long have I been holding Amy's hand? How long have I been holding on to her?

"I'm going to find more beer," she says.

And then she is gone.

I'm outside my house again. Breathless from the com- bination of the memory and the run. Tristan grins at me and pats me on the back. "Are you asthmatic?" he asks. "Or just really out of shape?"

I give him the finger to tell him exactly what I think.

"Careful, Ella. You never know; I might call the cops on you. Oh, these young teenage vandals and their need to climb trees and sing loud nursery rhymes."

I laugh. "Given that I live here," I say, pointing to the house, "I think I'm allowed to sing nursery rhymes as loudly as I want."

"With your voice, I honestly wouldn't be surprised

if the neighbors tried to sue, anyway."

I'm tempted to give him the finger again, but I resist. Because I am a mature, sophisticated young woman. "I bet your own tones are hardly dulcet."

He smiles and inches ever so close to me before breaking out into a rousing chorus of "We Will Rock You" by Queen. His voice is surprisingly good. Tuneful and smooth. He sings almost as well as Petal does. Almost, but not quite. Petal's singing can charm the birds out of the trees and fill you up with the satisfaction you usually only feel after eating Thanksgiving dinner. E's singing, while lovely, would only ever stir a sad man to tears.

He smirks when he's done and says, "So, will you let me rock you?"

"Maybe," I say, pausing for dramatic effect, "if you were the last guy on Earth."

He raises an eyebrow. "Believe it or not, that's not what I meant. I was trying to ask whether you want me to help you see how Amy actually felt before she died?"

I look away, straight to the space on my lawn where Amy lost her life. I let my eyes bore into the grass, remembering the way her black hair fanned across it that night. "I still don't think you know," I tell him, turning down his offer of help. "I'll see you tomorrow."

"Yeah," he says with a heavy sigh. "See you."

He tucks his hands into his pockets and wanders down my street. I watch him disappear into the meandering night before I head back inside, let the empty house swallow me whole. Sometimes I worry that one of these mornings it won't spit me out again.

Chapter Sixteen

I DON'T MAKE IT TO SCHOOL THE NEXT DAY. HIDING IN MY bed, pretending I'm in another house, on another planet, is much more fun. Mark calls four times and Petal calls six, but I don't know what to say to them, so I ignore my beeping phone and bury my face in my pillow. It makes it difficult to breathe, and that gives me something to concentrate on.

I spend the day by myself with nothing but the *in out in out in out in out in out* of my breathing. It amazes me that this is all we need to live, that this unsatisfactory process is all it takes for my body to keep on going.

When it hits three o'clock, though, I get out of my toasty-warm bed. The chilly autumn air hits me, raising goose bumps on my skin. I didn't go to school. There are no consequences for not going to school. But I have to go to the child care center, because if my mother forces me to go to therapy with Roger, it will give me lifelong emotional scars. And god knows I've already got enough of those.

When I arrive, Tristan and Heather are sitting on my favorite destroyed green bench. Talking. He moves his mouth in reply to whatever she's saying, but he's staring straight over her shoulder. At me.

Heather turns her head, probably to work out what he's looking at. She readjusts her floral blouse—how many does the woman have?—eyes narrowing when she sees me. I walk over to them slowly, deliberately. As if the ground beneath me is made of eggshells instead of concrete.

"Hi," I say to Heather.

Hate twists her face, screws with her features. She taps her watch. *Tap. Tap. Tap.* And I stand there defiant, because I know I'm two minutes early. "Cutting it close, Ella," she says finally. "Make sure you're always on time. Have you signed in at the front desk yet?"

She's trying to say, *Don't give me an excuse to get rid of you.* She's trying to say, *I don't need one.*

Can I really blame her for being so cold? I certainly didn't need an excuse to fuck up her son's life. Amy and I didn't need an excuse to steal his books, to snicker when he walked past, to mock his clothes.

She has every right to hate me.

"I'll make sure of it," I say, biting my tongue to hold

back an angry reply. "And yes, I have signed in. What would you like me to do today?"

"There's nothing specific that you can do," she says, her words clip-clopping out of her mouth. "Tristan's already going to be supervising the play area."

I look over to where the kids are sitting. Today instead of playing on the slide or chasing one another around, they're each kneading a piece of play dough. I guess once in a blue moon Heather decides they need to do an organized activity rather than be left to their own devices. She's like my mother that way.

"Maybe I could help him?"

"Tristan's not incompetent. *He* can manage twenty kids. Why don't you just make sure that Casey doesn't get into trouble? *No* idea why, but she really took a shine to you the other day."

Heather smiles, skin stretched tight. I don't respond, keep a poker face. The seconds tick by. One Mississippi, two Mississippi, three Mississippi . . . Her smile wavers. Before her lips can snap closed, I notice her teeth. Shiny, white. Pointy. She has fangs like a vampire. Like her son, Peter. It was one of the things we mercilessly teased him about.

"Okay. Sure, I'll make sure Casey stays out of trouble," I say, even though I'd much rather drive nails through my own palms.

Because spending time with Casey, who shares her doubts and dreams with me—and laughs like my dead best friend—is going to carve my insides out. By the time I leave here I'll be nothing but a hollow ache.

Shit. Maybe I really should see my mother's idiotic therapist.

I decide to read a story while Casey shapes her blob of play dough into a slightly more circular blob. I show her the book I've chosen. It's about a beetle's travels around a school playground or something.

"I'm ten," she says, picking up her piece of dough and throwing it back down onto the concrete. *Splat.* "I'm too freaking old for this."

I should tell her to watch her ten-year-old mouth. But I don't, can't, won't. She needs some way to express her anger. Everyone does.

Instead, I flick open the cover of the book and begin to read: "'Jonathan scampered through the sea of black school shoes. He wasn't sure why, suddenly, he was so small compared to his old friends.'"

I pause.

Okay. So the story's about a kid who gets transformed into a beetle. It's like Kafka's *Metamorphosis*, except it's clearly aimed at scaring the crap out of kids.

"'Jonathan decided he'd hide in the—'"

"Stop reading." Casey's voice rings out, quiet and loud, all at once. Her fingers have quit shaping the green play dough.

Snap. I close the book cover.

I can't refuse Casey. Just like I couldn't refuse Amy.

"Why?" I say. "What's wrong with the book?"

Her pudgy fingers lay into the dough again, pulling it in and out and in and out until it looks so grotesquely weird that I think this kid could have a career as a modern artist. "That beetle, right?" she says, flicking a piece of hair out of her eyes. "He, like, crawls all over the teacher's blackboard and stuff and no one smashes him or anything. And then he saves some other beetle, and 'the Forces of Good'"—she brings her green, dough-covered fingers up to form quote marks—"turn him back into a boy again."

She stabs her fingers into the play dough and looks up at me. There are purple bruises painted beneath her eyes. "I mean, as if that story could have a happy ending. That beetle would have been squished, you know? The ending is always too happy in books."

I blink.

Well, look at that. The kid's a nihilist. A nihilist who likes to dream of the future.

She grabs a stray stick from the ground and thwacks it into her creation. Then she slides some of the gunky green dough off the stick so that it's partially camouflaged within her little blob of dough. She smiles. Rocks back onto her heels and surveys it.

The girl should forget her lace-dress-clad mechanic dream. She's definitely a crazy modern artist in the making.

Explosive Boy's walking around now, asking the kids what their blobs are meant to be. It turns out that most of them have been molding their nightmares.

"The bogeyman."

"A haunted house."

"My neighbor. Swear to god, he weighs, like, three hundred and fifty pounds."

My stomach twists as Explosive Boy wanders closer, closer, closer to Casey. His shadow blossoms over the gravely concrete where we're sitting. I look up. The sun ignites his hair from behind, turning it a stunning shade of pinky orange.

"What have you made?" Explosive Boy asks Casey. He's got that quiet kindness I noticed in him on the first day. I still think it's weird as hell that he can be this person, this Kid Whisperer, this guy who hands Kleenex to crying girls he doesn't know.

I don't get how he can be that person and still smell like gunpowder, still have the kind of temper that flares up into a bonfire. The kind of temper that made him punch one of my best friends earlier this week.

"Casey?" Tristan prompts when she doesn't reply.

"It's okay," I say. "If you don't want to tell us what it is—"

But her lips are moving; it's just that her words are too quiet to break out into the world.

"Pardon me," Explosive Boy says, and I jump a bit because, seriously? *Pardon me?*

"I couldn't quite hear you," he's saying to Casey. "Could you please repeat yourself?"

"It's me," Casey says, soft but audible. "I made myself."

Tristan's whole face unravels. He looks winded, his shock spilling into the air. "It's very . . ." He trails off, unsure of what to say. "Very good," he finally manages.

"Abstract." Why I'm helping him out, I don't know.

Maybe it's because I'm thinking that Casey has more in common with my dead best friend than a laugh.

"Yeah," Tristan says. "You could be a great. Like Picasso."

Casey flicks her fringe out of her brown eyes. She gingerly lifts her green creation. "Did Picasso look like this, too?"

My heart breaks, because she's ten and this question is real.

"Yeah," I say. "But you're way prettier. Unfaithful self-portrait, much?" Too loud. Too cheery. Too warm. My voice is so fucking unnatural.

I'm blaming it on Tristan's hair.

"Thanks," Casey says, tossing me the word like a dog bone. Like she doesn't believe it at all.

My attempt to comfort her crashes, burns, and dies.

"I need the bathroom," she says, standing. She wanders off toward the building behind us.

I fold my hands and lean forward so that I'm staring at my lap. At the ground. I try, through the sheer intensity of my gaze, to burrow my way into the asphalt. To bury myself. In the ground. Where Amy is.

I could find her.

And then someone's hand is on my shoulder, the fingers so sharp they send volts of electricity spiraling through me. One, two, three, four, five.

It's him, of course.

Hey there, Tristan.

"Are you thinking about *her*?"

I put myself together, stitch a smile across my face. "Yeah, I've been getting all reflective about how very fucking awesome Heather is."

He frowns. "Be serious."

"Well, who did *you* mean?" I ask, pretending to be shocked by his response.

"Amy. You know, you don't have to do this—"

"Oh," I say, "but I do. These children *need* me."

And something in my voice, something about my

playful tone, must get to him. Because he doesn't bother with more words. Just sighs and leaves me there, still holding the fucked-up creation that's supposed to represent Casey's self.

Thankfully, Casey comes back from the bathroom before I can unleash my wrath on a defenseless blob of play dough. She resettles herself on the ground beside me. We both watch Tristan's retreating back. "When my dad acts like that," she says, "my mom always asks him why the fuck he has PMS."

It surprises me how easily her lips curved around the word. It surprises me that the word, the Big Bad word that Heather banned me from using in front of these kids, fits like a glove in Casey's mouth.

It surprises me, even though it shouldn't.

Amy was like that, too. She had parents who dropped those words all over the house. Amy's home was a land mine of bad language. Arguments would break out in the kitchen while we were watching the Disney channel.

Goddamnit

Absolute shit

Go fuck yourself, Ted.

Sometimes Amy was the one at the center of all the angry words.

That fat bitch.

And she never knew that I knew that when she buried her face in the imported cushions, she was crying.

"Casey," I say, "you shouldn't use words like that."

She looks up at me. "Why?"

"Because," I say, pretending to be the wholesome girl I'm not, "they're bad."

But Casey has decoded the lack of conviction in my voice. She smiles, and she looks so much like Amy. She stands, holds up her blob of a creation, and opens her mouth nice and wide, ready to defy me.

"Casey, please don't," I say quickly. "Heather will kick me out of here if you say that loud enough for her to hear."

Snap. Her mouth closes. *She must like me then.* A grin breaks loose on her face. Her eyes sparkle, like an actress in one of those old movies. "Fuck," she whispers conspiratorially, and she's so pleased with herself.

Pink runs across her cheeks, makes the purple beneath her eyes less noticeable. Her whole posture changes: shoulders rolled back, straightened. Her nose gets tipped up in the air. Her profile is sharp and brimming with life against the endless sky.

"I like that word," she says.

I resist the temptation to hug Casey, to try to squeeze out the things that haunt her. I close my eyes against the sight of this girl who is so much like my best friend.

And because I can't take it anymore, I say to Casey, "I have to go." I whisper, "Good-bye."

And then I'm crashing back into the building and through the automatic glass front doors. Out onto the street. Hopefully my mother's "donating" too much money for Heather to fire me over this.

The wind bites into me, and I feel even colder than usual. I wrap my arms around myself and slowly begin the walk home.

Chapter Seventeen

MY MOTHER HAS LEFT MY BREAKFAST ON THE KITCHEN counter. A slice of toast slathered with avocado and a tall, skinny glass of orange juice. I slide the plate away from me. Eye it suspiciously. I can't remember the last time my mother made me breakfast. Or the last time there was orange juice in our house.

And fuck, she's even left me a note on the fridge saying that she's glad about my progress at the child care center. Guess Heather hasn't told her about yesterday's walkout yet. My mother hopes—or so her neat handwriting tells me—that I have a nice day. At school.

I snort. It's a Saturday. Mom's seven-days-a-week job means she sometimes loses track of the time.

Well, never fear, Mother, I'll have a nice day. Just not at school.

Someone's already at the barn when I get there. Someone's already standing in its very center, in the midst of all the bales of hay. A tall figure in a faded, red hoodie and jeans so soft and old that they look as if they're about to fall apart.

A tall figure with firebrand hair. Tristan.

He's got his back to me and his earbuds in his ears. So I clear my throat as loudly as possible. He turns, eyes widening with surprise. "Hi," he says, getting rid of the earbuds and giving me his maple syrup smile. "What are you doing here?"

"I was about to ask you the same thing," I say, walking over to him.

His shrug is casual. Too casual. "It's a good spot to think."

I smile and add, "Plus no one thinks to look for teenage delinquents in a fucking barn, because seriously, what could we even do here, right?"

He raises his eyebrows. "Well, you promised me orgies . . . but I'm assuming you're actually here to do a Pick Me Up." His mouth twists as if he's tasted something bitter when he talks about Pick Me Ups. "Where are the other musketeers?"

"I have no idea. Burning down a house maybe."

He doesn't laugh. Instead, he sighs and presses a hand to his forehead. "Yeah." He's silent for a moment, then he says, "Some Brittany girl has apparently been telling everyone that I burn things."

I knew it was only a matter of time before Brittany's shit got back to him.

"Do you?" I ask, flopping onto a bale of hay. I reach into my pocket and pull out my phone and fumble with the buttons. Finally, I manage to send a single-word message to Mark.

Barn.

He'll be here in less than ten minutes. He always is. And Pet will be with him.

"Do I what?" Tristan asks.

I shrug, pick up a bit of hay, and twirl it in my fingers, examining it to make sure there's no pigeon poo on it. I slide the hay into my mouth and chew, chew, chew. As if I'm chewing the misery out of the world. I don't know if I'm ready to ask him this question yet.

He whacks the hay out of my hand. "That's cow food," he says. "You're a human. You don't have six stomachs."

I roll my eyes. "Thanks for that little piece of information. Really illuminating."

"You know what else would be illuminating? If you told me what *the hell you're asking me*."

There's no way to phrase my question delicately. So I choose to avoid asking it at all. "Do you . . . want to go home?" I say instead. "It's pretty obvious you don't like Pick Me Ups."

I mean, there's no reason for him to be here. He freaked out so badly after the bridge and when I jumped from the third floor and when I almost fell from the tree. I'm giving him an out. If he wants it. Because I'm sick of being a bitch.

"No."

"But—why?"

He sweeps some hay aside, absentmindedly traces the letter E in the dirt beneath it. Runs his fingers through those lines over and over again. "You saved my life," he says eventually. "We're not really even. I want us to be even."

He's such a bad liar. "You're lying," I say. "You're fucking lying. Don't stay because you feel sorry for me. I don't need your pity."

I don't need anyone's pity.

"Well, you don't fucking have it, okay? God." He stands up, puts some distance between us. "You're insane; did you know that? Are you always like this?"

"Like what?" I don't bother answering the question about my sanity.

"Hypocritical."

"What do you mean?"

"You weren't going to ask me about going home. What did you really want to say, _you_ fucking liar?"

I glower at him. Fine, if he wants to hear it, I'll say it.

"Do you like burning things?" Deadpan voice. Deadpan eyes.

He shakes his head. "Are you being serious?"

Suddenly, all I want to do is take the question back, pull my words back inside me and keep them locked away forever. I hear Heather on repeat in my head: *You're a horrible person, you're a horrible person, you're a horrible person.*

And shit, she's right. Even when I'm trying to be nice, I'm an asshole.

Tristan runs a hand through his hair. "Look," he says. "Just because it's red. Does. Not. Make. Me. An. Arsonist."

"But you are an arse," says another voice.

Mark knows how to make an entrance. Most beautiful girl in a five-mile radius on his arm, witty comeback line on his lips.

And Petal, shit. I'm still amazed that this goddess of a girl ever chose to hang out with me. She belongs with the perfect girls. The ones who drive expensive cars and don't jump off buildings, or break into supermarkets, or hang out with boys who smell like gunpowder. Thank god for her extreme misanthropy, her hatred of all social bullshit and the mind games those perfect girls seem to play with each other in Sherwood.

"What's up?" Petal asks.

What's up is that their timing is perfect. What's up is

that if I had to stand here for even another minute with Explosive Boy, having this conversation, my ego would have taken some serious hits.

"What's up is I need a Pick Me Up." I say the words before I can think, because we're in the barn.

Because I need a distraction.

I want to ask Mark about the image of me and Amy in my backyard, her hand slipping away from mine. But I want to do that when we're alone. Letting Tristan and Pet in on a memory of mine isn't something I'm eager to do.

Not that Mark will tell me anything, anyway.

For a second I contemplate getting Mark really high to loosen his tongue.

Of course, there are a hundred buts, a hundred reasons why I should never do that.

But what if I need to?

If I knew the truth, I wouldn't have to hurt anymore. My head wouldn't hurt; my heart wouldn't hurt; my body—

So tired. My knees buckle a little. I imagine the joints creaking like an old wooden door.

And then someone's hand is in front of my face, and I can see fingers. I can see space, air in between the fingers, stretching out forever. It's there, an image that bobs and floats. But at the same time it's not there. . . . I can't feel anything. . . .

"Hello? Anybody home?" Tristan says.

I stare, trying to dredge up a response. But there isn't anything to say. There is just the heaviness that has seeped into my bone marrow.

Hands. On my shoulders. Shake, shake, shake.

Feeling washes over me. My head breaks the surface of the water I was under.

Shake. It's Tristan. He's shaking me into the moment.

I push his hand away and force a smile that I instantly regret.

I don't want him to know me. I don't. But judging by the way his eyebrows are colliding, he already knows something about me that not many people do. That sometimes, even when I'm awake, I fall so far inside myself that I'm almost asleep.

And I'm not sure what else to do, so I stick my hands in my pockets and take a small step toward the staircase. Because I know how to jump. I know how to feel the wind in my hair, how to let it rip all other thoughts from my mind.

"Ella. Seriously. Another freaking Pick Me Up? I told you that you're doing it all wrong. You guys are just giving yourselves adrenaline rushes. Amy wouldn't have felt that way before she died."

Tristan is too logical, too sensible for us. I bet he likes calculus.

"Shut up," Mark snarls. "Shut up. What would you know?"

"A lot! You're not the only one who's experienced the death of someone close. Why the hell are you doing this? Do you want to lose someone else? Because you know, ultimately, that's where this goes."

Pet replies before Mark can. The sneer in her voice, in her eyes, creeps over the entire barn until even the bales of hay seem contemptuous. "Are you afraid of dying?"

And Tristan burns up the contempt with two words: "Fuck, yes!"

We're all silent after that. Tristan is exploding against us like I'd hoped he would.

Except he's not driving us together. Well, he may be driving Mark and Pet together; but I'm standing here in total silence, stuffing bits of hay into my mouth and whistling to avoid this conversation.

The dreamlike state is gone. I feel every word of this conversation. Every. Fucking. Word. Every word is my two best friends not telling me the truth. Lying to me. Every word hurts. Every word punches me in the gut.

"Look, it's up to Ella," Petal's saying. "She's a big girl. If she wants to jump off shit, then that's her business. I'll make sure she doesn't die, just like she would for me."

All eyes on me. Spotlight. I take a deep breath and— lights, camera, action. I take another step, and as my foot crunches down into the hay, my resolve breaks. Not because I'm scared. But because it's just not enough anymore.

"I don't want to jump off anything right now." To tell the truth, it's getting a little stale. Jump off this, jump off that, jump off shit. It's the same feeling, the same roar in your ears no matter where you fall from.

I want something different. Like floating facedown in a river and almost drowning. Scary, but so exhilarating.

My eyes lock onto the old dartboard in the corner of the room. Amy stole it from the teachers' lounge when we were in ninth grade because someone dared her to. She gave it to me for my birthday that year since she didn't have a clue what else to do with it.

And when she died, I put it in the barn. Just like Petal hung the scarves and dresses she "borrowed" from Amy over the safety railings.

Just like Mark hung all her vinyls on the walls. That was their thing as a couple. He and Amy liked their retro rock, their indie rock, their heavy metal, and their sleepy-town Beatles tunes. Their romance floated along in an octopus's garden, in a yellow submarine.

A breeze murmurs through the barn, stirring a million whispers in the hay. The vinyls spin and scratch against the walls. My friends' eyes are still on me. My silence is getting too long. It's stretching out forever. I wait and wait for someone to reach out and snap it, smash it to pieces.

But they all seem to be waiting for me.

So I close my eyes and say what's on my mind. I point at the dartboard, at the space it occupies between two of Amy's favorite vinyls: Hendrix at Woodstock and one of Led Zeppelin's live recordings.

"Yes, Ella?" Mark asks.

Apparently, pointing at a dartboard and choking on an explanation leads to questions in an awkward tone. I jab my finger again, swallow the porcupine in my throat. "I want you to throw darts at *me*."

When I say it, their eyes get so wide. Wider than saucers, saucepans. Their mouths hang open as if they're cartoon characters, as if the dentist has just said, "Open up, please."

But there are still scribbles of sparkle in their eyes. Still bits of light that yell "Yeah, we're game." Tristan smells more like gunpowder than he ever has; but I know, I just know that Mark and Pet are going to help me do this.

Because they're idiots.

Because they love me, even though they're lying to me.

Chapter Eighteen

"*E*LLA, ARE YOU SURE?"

My back is pressed against the wooden wall of the barn. Mark's toying with a piece of red chalk, tossing it from hand to hand. "Are you sure?" he asks again in his lazy drawl. He knows I'm not backing down. Not now.

Amy would've kept on going.

Mark sweeps the chalk around me in a wide arc until I'm encased in a red chalk bubble. I stretch my arms and touch the sides of the bubble, shuffle my feet outward until they're at the edges of the red line, too. My head sinks lower, and my hair shifts up behind me, pressed against the wall.

"Okay, guys," I call. "I'm ready for target practice."

"Ella—" It's Tristan. He's holding a dart in his hand, and he's got this look on his face. I told him he could go—again—and he didn't reply, but he hasn't gone anywhere. Yet. I'm certain that once the darts start flying at me, he'll fly out the door. "Are you sure you really want to do this?" he asks.

"Stop confusing me. I'm up for it." When he shakes his head, my mind starts racing. There's only so much you can do before a person rats you out. If Tristan tells anyone—my parents, the school—I'm fucked. "Look, Tristan, this is really *safer* than me jumping off things. I mean, even if one of the darts hits me, they don't look like they could kill."

He raises his eyebrows and turns the dart over in his hands. His eyes linger on the sharp metallic tip. Okay, so what if he has a point? So what if they look totally dangerous? They're *not* going to kill me.

Because I'm a fucking teenager. And because we've set this up so that the gnome's watching me from the third floor. And it's highly unlikely that my best friend and I are both going to die in front of the same garden gnome.

"Besides," I say, feeling a need to justify myself out loud, "I can get back more of my memory like this—"

I stop speaking before I finish the sentence, because this is the first time I've mentioned getting my memories back. My hand wants to slap itself over my mouth, take back the words.

I can't. They sit in a nest of hay.

Mouths agape.

"You mean—" Petal says. "You mean you're remembering stuff from that night?" Panic flickers like something flammable in her voice. I'm amazed the entire barn doesn't go up in a blaze.

I close my eyes. What's so bad that she's *this scared* for me to find out about it? What terrible thing are they hiding from me?

My chest constricts. My deep breaths shallow out. I dig my nails into my wrist to keep myself in the moment.

Wake up, Ella. Wake up. This is not the time to go under.

I choke out a response. "Yeah. Remember, I asked you where I was when Amy died?" It was one of the first things I said to Petal when she came out of her room.

"Yeah, but I just don't know. I mean, you spent most of the night with Amy."

She stops speaking and exchanges a look with Mark. And I realize that Mark had said that no one knew where Amy was later that night, that no one had seen her.

Except Petal saw her, apparently. Petal saw her *with me*.

And now I really can't breathe. The air tastes like poison.

Where was I when Amy died?

My hand forms a fist. I slam it into the wooden barn wall behind me. I gasp as the hot pain spreads through my knuckles. And then I laugh at myself. Nothing's even broken. I'm being such a freaking scaredy-cat.

"Just throw the dart already!"

Well, nothing's broken *yet*.

Petal goes first. And there's something angry in the way she tosses her dart. She leans back like the pitcher in a baseball game, and she throws. Adrenaline rushes through my body, floods the fingertips I've splayed against the wall. Fight or flight. Fight or flight.

My body's telling me to run from the sharp, quivering point of a dart buried about two inches away from me. But for once my mind's overpowering my body and I'm yelling, "Is that all you've got? Come on, bring it. Bring it!"

And Mark does. He's a bit more coordinated than Petal; and when the dart slams into the triangle of space between my underarm and side, he whoops. "Ten points to me!"

"This isn't a competition, you idiot. We're not playing a game." And that's Tristan, being sensible. Probably wondering what the fuck he got himself into by accepting my invitation to play Pick Me Ups back in English Lit.

But the rest of their argument is lost to me. I can hear the dart quivering, bass vibrations thrumming through the wood, through the air. They sink into my ears and take me back, take me back to the bass beat at the party.

"Good vibrations," Amy says. We're passing some guy who's doing hip thrusts like this is the fucking seventies.

He jives toward me, and I remember that he sits next to me in Bio. I give him a weak smile.

"Ella, baby—"

Before he can finish the sentence, I whack him lightly in the chest. "I know you're drunk, and I know you know that I'm drunk." I wait for this confusing sentence to sink in. When he shakes his head as if to dislodge water from his ears, I figure he's processed. "But you're still not getting lucky. Don't embarrass yourself trying."

"Okay." He nods gratefully.

I've let him down easy. Most people who call me "baby" get slapped. I'm not anyone's baby. I belong to myself.

And then Amy laughs and tugs me farther down the hall. "You're such a heartbreaker." Her voice sloshes in my eardrums like the punch in our cups earlier. The punch from when we were playing twenty questions.

I remember what I said and feel my soul, feel it dropping into my feet along with my drunk heart.

"Ella," she says. We've reached the second floor of my house.

"Ella," Amy repeats. Her hand waves slowly through the air in front of my face. Her fingers slide across my vision, and for a second it's like I'm seeing the world through shutters. Like I'm semiblind.

"Yeah?" I say. "Did you find Pet earlier?"

"Yeah," she says. "Yeah. She was dancing on your parents' precious dining-room table. You know Petal."

Yep. She's a show-off. Knows how to dance and flaunts it.

Amy laughs again. She's laughing a lot; but her face is crumpling *in on itself, and I know she's gone too far. I know* we've *gone too far with the alcohol this time.*

"I lost her again, though," Amy says. "You lose Mark?"

I nod. "Yeah, I did," I say. "Amy, that thing he said before——"

Her voice is sharp; but laughter, drunk and loose, blows beneath its surface. Slurred, blurred words. "About liking me better when I was fat? That thing?" She laughs, but the sound breaks apart like a smashed beer bottle.

We step through the darkness, and the shards crack and crack and crack in Amy's laughter until there's no laughter left. She asks as we put our feet onto the second staircase, "Did you like me better then, too, Ella? Did you?"

"To me you're still the same person."

I realize——too late——that this is the wrong thing to say. She wants to have changed, to have become better. Freshman and sophomore years weren't just about losing her weight; they were about losing her personality——her lame, geeky personality.

How much of this running around and breaking into shopping centers at midnight shit is her? How much of it is her making herself up?

Who is *my best friend?*

It doesn't really matter, because I don't even know who I am. What matters is that I love her and that she's shattering right in front of me. I take her hand and whisper as we ascend the stairs. "It's okay, Ames. It's okay. We loved you then and we loved you now. Always will."

And then we reach the top of the stairs, the top floor of my house. It should be silent, because I've warned everyone to stay away from here or else face annihilation. But the darkness has a certain animalistic breath. It reeks of alcohol even worse than Amy and me.

"Oi," I say, spotting a black shadow shape in the corner against the door of my parents' bedroom. "Who's there?"

The couple leaps apart, jumping as if my words are flames burning guilt into their skin.

I can't believe it: Mark and Pet. Staring back at us.

As of this moment, I want *their guilt to burn them.*

"Amy," Mark begins, taking a step toward us. "Amy, I can expl—"

She's gone, slipping away from me, from us, again. Splintering heels on stairs. Sob, sob, sob. It sounds as if each of the steps is cracking beneath Amy's feet.

I stare at Mark and Petal. "What the fuck are you doing?" I ask them.

Mark said he could explain. Please, God, let him be able to explain.

I open my eyes. Another dart zooms into the space next to my belly. I feel sick again. I'm surprised to see Tristan with his arm raised, ready to throw his dart. He's too far away to be able to see my face fall, tumbling like a house of cards.

"STOP!" I yell. "STOP!"

Because if Mark has an explanation, I want to hear it *right now*.

Chapter Nineteen

*H*E DOES HAVE AN EXPLANATION, BUT IT'S SO UNBE-
lievable I don't know if I ever want to talk to him again.

I look up at the gnome. Swallow, find my voice.

"What were you on? Both of you. What the fuck made
you think kissing Pet would help you figure out how to
make Amy happy?"

Mark cradles his head in his hands and rocks back and
forth. "I'm an idiot," he moans.

"Me, too," Petal says. "Such a fucking idiot."

"In more ways than one," Tristan says to Petal. "I
mean, you could do a lot better than him."

I swear, Tristan's jokes always come at ridiculously
inappropriate moments. I glare him into silence, meet the
eyes of my two best friends in the world, and say, "What
happened that night? What else happened that you don't
want to tell me about?"

"Nothing."

But like always, there is something so stilted about the way Mark says it. He's lying. He's been lying all along, and his story is finally starting to unravel. Like a thread from the end of a T-shirt, if I pull and pull and pull, all the lies will eventually fall out.

For instance, he still hasn't answered my question about why in god's name he thought "kissing lessons" from Petal were a good idea. This shit about not being able to "please" Amy and thinking he needed some practice is completely insane. I need to keep pulling at that thread.

"Seriously? Nothing? Where was I, then? When Amy died? Was I with you or Pet?"

The questions pour out of my mouth. Black and ugly and impossible to run from. Like tar on the surface of a road. I force myself to pause, to wait for the answers.

"I don't know where you were—" And it feels like the millionth time that I've received this bullshit answer. He looks at Pet, and she shakes her head, too.

"I don't know, either," she says.

I'm probably imagining things. I hope I'm imagining things. But for a second there it seriously looked like Mark's eyes widened, that he warned Petal off saying something. I look from one to the other, trying to find the secret that lies between them.

Petal's fingers twist in and out of one another. She's always been a bad liar.

"Amy was pissed off at us for what we did. She ran off, and none of us saw her after that."

But now she's tearing a piece of hay to pieces. She can't even look at me.

I want to shout that she's lying, that it's not true. But a broken image comes to me. I hear their echoing voices chasing me down the stairs as I chased after Amy.

My head falls into my hands. My palms attempt to rub the wrinkles from my forehead. Why can't I remember any more? What is my mind refusing to show me? What are they refusing to tell me?

I thought our friendship was worth more.

But then I remember Amy, how far we let her go; and I wonder whether these friendships were ever really as strong as I thought they were if we were ignoring stuff like that.

If we were ignoring Amy never getting a tray in the cafeteria. Amy looking hollow, looking like a coffin. Like death.

And then an idea hits me, and my heart feels as if it's sitting at the bottom of my belly. What if I *was* with her when she jumped?

"Was I—" My words are swallowed into my stomach, too. I want to sink to the floor and stay there, but I don't. I remain standing. I enunciate slowly and carefully. "Was I with her when she—you know?"

They stare back at me, stricken. I'm not sure whether it's because I've found out their secret or whether it's because they're just shocked at the idea. My stomach twists, spins like a hurricane. My heart is caught up in the eye of the storm.

Mark swallows. "No," he says. "No, no way. You couldn't have been."

"Why not?"

"Because we would have seen you on the roof when we ran out. And you weren't; you were on the ground with us."

Except. I can climb down that tree in less than a minute. I could have met them on the ground, and no one would have known. Everyone who saw me that night saw me looking at her body, thought I was flaking apart. Crumbling.

The photos show me white-faced with bloodshot eyes, sobbing, hair sticking out at weird angles. And my hands. In the pictures, my hands look like blurs, because I couldn't stop them from shaking.

What if that reaction wasn't just grief?

But I say, "Okay." Because accepting what Mark's saying makes it easier to get up and walk around the barn. It makes it easier to pick up my thoughts, pluck them out of the hay, and arrange them. Annotate them like I do my homework.

"I still don't get it, Mark. What were you on?"

He shakes his head. "Only pot. Jason gave it to me," he says. "Petal wasn't on anything that I'm aware of."

"Just drunk," she says. She's crying. Not those noisy sobs that demand attention but this quiet kind of crying. Almost as if her soul is washing away with her tears.

This isn't all there is to it. I can just feel it. I can see it in the way Mark scuffs his shoe across the ground and darts his eyes from piece of hay to piece of hay. He refuses to look at me, and I won't look at anything except him and Petal.

And she's still not looking at me, either.

Why is it that my two best friends won't look at me and the random new kid will? Why is it that Tristan's staring at me with this weird expression on his face? As if he thinks my mind is a puzzle that he can work out if he concentrates hard enough.

But my mind is not a puzzle. Like everyone else's mind, it's a fucking maze. Twist, turn, twist, turn . . . turn, turn, twist. No matter how hard Tristan tries to delve into my mind he's going to get lost. Because god knows I feel lost inside my own head, and if I can't sort this shit out then no one else can, either.

And Mark is still looking at the ground, at his shoe-laces. And Petal is looking at Mark's shoelaces, too, and her chipped red nail polish and the roof of the barn. She starts humming some goddamn country song, and oh, my god.

Oh, my god.

I'm not sure I can handle them kissing each other the night Amy died. Because I've been blaming myself, but what if it wasn't me? What if it was *them*?

Does it even matter who or what it was? Nothing changes the fact that Amy became a scribble on my front lawn. All of us still ignored the fact that she was breaking until it was too late. Nothing will ever change that.

I'm crying like Pet now. Crying and pacing, trying to gather my thoughts. But for each thought that I slot into position, more thoughts escape, slip through the strands of my hair and through the hay like smoke.

"I need—"

Cut-off sentence, disappearing along with my jumbled thoughts. I don't know what I need; I don't fucking know.

I can't take it anymore. The silence, the tense, fucking silence that Mark and Pet refuse to break with the truth. They're not going to tell me. I know they're not going to tell me, so what's the point?

Screw this.

So I do what I seem to be doing a lot of these days when things get hard. I leave.

I walk straight out the door, past a shocked Mark, Pet, and Tristan. I pick up pieces of hay, fragments of thought, as I walk. And then I'm out of the barn, away from their scrutiny. The sky examines me; and I continue, wandering, sorting through the bouquet of hay bunched in my hands.

I walk down the winding path toward town. Then I change my mind and walk back in the other direction. And I break into a run, because it's the only thing I know how to do. Run and jump off things and do my homework.

The thump of my feet against the ground. The *thwack* of shoes against dirt. It should feel like something; it should send vibrations curling up my legs. But it's too much; it's all too much, and I can barely breathe right now, let alone feel anything.

And then someone yells, "Hey, wait up!"

I stop. Because I'm dumb like that, listening to people and shit. I turn to see who it is. Again, because I'm stupid. It's Tristan. I want to groan; I want to keep running until I'm just *away*.

"Ella!"

Something in his voice stops me. It's so—raw. My name's exposed like a broken cord, a copper wire twisting out from the black rubber.

And it stops me, and he sprints toward me doing his whole bullet-run again. I know he can't stop himself, so I dodge to one side to prevent him from barreling into me. He manages to stop by wrapping an arm around a stop sign.

He breathes heavily, hands on knees. He stares up at

me with those pretty hazel eyes, waiting for me to speak, but I have nothing to say. Nothing.

"How you doing?" is what eventually comes out. Just like at the tree the other day.

"Fine, fine." He runs a hand through his explosive hair. Straightens up. His breathing evens out. "It's not me who just discovered a petty love affair that occurred on the night of her best friend's death."

I punch him in a jokey way but still hard, because I'm goddamn pissed. "Yeah. And don't use that cheesy voice again or else I will *actually* hurt you." I do a few threatening uppercuts, fists slicing through blue sky, almost reaching the fluffy clouds.

Mark did this exact same thing when we were walking through the park on our way back from the bridge.

It seems like eons ago. Everything was hanging by a thread then. I had a feeling that they were hiding something, but now I *know* that I was right. And I know some of what they were hiding.

Now that thread has been snipped. Now everything feels broken.

I can't trust them anymore.

What else are they keeping from me?

Nothing. That's what Mark said. But it was one of his sideways words.

I look up from my shoes and find Tristan staring at me.

"What?" I start to move once more. Walking instead of running. I'm giving him time to get his breath back, and he knows it. A ridiculous grin lights up his face.

"What?" I snap at him again.

"What?" He echoes me like a parrot, head tilted to one side, chin jutting out like a crazy violinist's. "Where are you going, is what I was going to ask."

"Oh. Right. Um, I want to go to Ghost Town if that's okay with you." This is my way of admitting that I want him to come with me. That I don't want to be alone.

Because all the kids clear out of Ghost Town once it gets dark.

"Ghost Town?"

I sigh. Must this boy have everything explained to him? "The other side of the river. There're a couple of abandoned houses there."

"Seriously?" he asks. "All those houses on the other side of the river are abandoned?"

"Yeah. Don't worry, there are no ghosts."

He laughs, but I notice the way his fingers slide into the pockets of his jeans. I see his thumbs, pressing hard against the material. White, drained of blood. I wonder if he's imagining Ethan's ghost creaking through the Ghost Town houses.

I know I'm imagining Amy's.

I've already started steering us toward Ghost Town when I remember that I left the gnome with Mark and Petal. I'm tempted to run all the way back up this gray, winding path to the barn just to get it. Because the gnome is my ref. The gnome is my safety blanket.

And without the gnome? Everything feels unstable.

I want to reach out and latch on to Tristan, bury my fingers in his jacket to regain my balance. But I know it's emotional balance I'm lacking, not physical. So I gulp down air and keep walking.

"Why are you coming with me?"

He meets my eyes, and I hate him for it. I hate him for his ability to *look at me*. Because my best friends won't even look at me.

"I told you I was going to help you find out what Amy felt like. And I meant it."

I put my hands on my hips. It's taking every last piece of resolve I have to keep my barriers up, to keep my tone harsh. "Well, you don't seem too into Pick Me Ups. What do you propose?"

He's unfazed. He plucks some hay from the bouquet I'm still holding. Steals one of my thoughts and slides it into his mouth. He puffs on the hay as if it's a cigarette, or a pipe and he's Sherlock fucking Holmes. Solving the mystery of my best friend's suicide.

Or was it even that? The police were convinced, the

ambulance people were convinced. But we didn't have to physically push Amy. Word after word after word could have prodded and poked her onto the precipice.

Snap. Her neck breaking in the weeds.

It's not just sticks and stones that break bones like everyone seems to think. Words break bones from the inside out. They sink into our bloodstream, into our bone marrow and eat away at us.

They break bones. They break hearts. They break souls.

And we're still walking. And Tristan's still puffing away on his cigarette-hay. And the sky is still blue, and the world still feels gray.

"Tristan?" I want him to speak, to say something because I don't want to think anymore. "What do you propose? How can I really feel like Amy?"

I carry on a few short steps before I realize he's stopped walking. Curious, I turn around, the bouquet of hay—my gathered thoughts—clutched to my chest like a shield as I wait for his answer.

He takes the hay out of his mouth and twirls it between his palms. I watch it, watch him. "Pick Me Ups make you feel a rush, right? They make you feel high?"

I give a small nod.

"Do you honestly think Amy felt high when she was about to die?"

He's said similar things before, but not in this voice.

Not like this. Not so that it actually registered.

This. It hits me in the gut. Winds me. Of course not. Of course she didn't feel high when she was about to die.

"Suicide isn't about an adrenaline rush."

He's so right. It's not. It's about the opposite. It's about the feeling I get when I'm coming down from a Pick Me Up. The sludgy black tar that tears at my intestines. The poison that seems to fill the air.

Adrenaline rushes are addictive. Suicide is not addictive, not at all.

But I stand my ground and stare at Tristan over the space that separates us. "What," I ask, "do you propose?"

"It's a surprise," he says, tapping his nose. "You'll just have to wait and see. On Monday, after work."

Chapter Twenty

AT MIDNIGHT I FIND MYSELF SLIDING OPEN MY BEDroom window. The tree next to it, the one that brushes up against the side of the house at certain points, has become a close friend this month. I stand on the window ledge and step onto one of the lower branches, fastening my fingers around a branch that floats overhead.

Soon I've swung myself up onto that branch. Then the one above it. The one above that.

And now I'm on the roof. I'm on the roof, and I can see the spot Amy must have jumped from, because she took some of the tiles on the edge with her.

From up here you can see the entire street, the houses that glow like furnaces in the dark. Occasionally, in some of the uncurtained windows, silhouettes dance into my line of vision. But I don't come up here for the view.

I come up here to close my eyes and imagine surfing down the sloping roof, tiles falling away beneath my feet. I come here to imagine smashing into weeds just like Amy did.

A moth settles on my skin, and my eyes flicker open, flicker over to the patch of grass on my front lawn where my best friend died.

I asked my parents if we could move somewhere else after it happened. But Mom told me to stop being ridiculous. We'd have to wait a few years, at least, before it would be worth selling the house. No one wants to buy a house where a girl has died. Especially not for a premium price.

The putter of an engine cuts the still night air. A silver Lexus peels down the street and pulls up directly in front of our house. Dad. He's getting out of the car now. Most of his face is shadowed, but weak moonlight dips over the tip of his nose. He starts toward the house, his shoes *thushing* against the damp grass.

He stops just before he reaches the front door, on the porch. He sighs and stares at the door for three heartbeats' time. And then he's heading back toward the car, opening the door, and climbing in. Once inside, he stares at the house. A man torn.

I keep waiting for him to notice me standing on the roof. Keep waiting for him to wave. But he doesn't. So I creep across the roof and climb through the tangle of tree limbs, touching down in the garden.

But before I can walk out from beneath the shadows

of the tree, I hear the engine rev. I start running, but it's too late—the Lexus is already streaking up the street at a dangerous speed. Dad has always driven too fast.

Except for when he was driving me to basketball practice. Then he was the world's most responsible driver. I remember how he always insisted on playing the worst music on the way there, and how to make up for it he'd always take me for Mexican on the way back.

I wander to the middle of the yard. Bite my lip.

I never thought I would feel anything if my parents were out of my life. After all, it's not like they've paid much attention to me since I hit my teens. But seeing Dad drive away like that, something knifes through my chest.

I look down at my feet. Dead, moonlit leaves curl around them. I watch the leaves until an icy wind blows them away, and then I climb back up to the roof, where I sit, waiting for god knows what. At two o'clock in the morning I unpeel my dry lips and scream at the sky.

Chapter Twenty-one

ON MONDAY, BLOODY MONDAY, WHEN I GET TO THE CHILD care center after school, Peter is there, standing behind the front desk. Peter. Peter, who somehow got up the courage to ask Amy out that one time, and she threw back her head and laughed her scorn for all the world to hear. I laughed along with her.

Peter. Is. Fucking. Here.

Just when you think you can forget about the old you. Just when you think you can try to be someone better, along comes fucking Peter Paton to remind you of just how bad you were. *Are.*

He's got his back turned. He hasn't seen me yet. I want to keep it that way.

But I have to go over there and sign in for my shift.

Step. Step. Step.

I'm dragging this out unnecessarily because he's already turned around and locked eyes with me. He doesn't react, doesn't smile or grin or nod or shout a greeting, and that kills me. It kills me inside, because the Peter I knew, the one who arrived at our school not so long ago, that boy had a smile for everyone.

I reach the desk. Force a smile at him.

He doesn't acknowledge it. Doesn't even acknowledge that he knows me. But he stares at me. Stares at me and stares at me and stares at me as I write my name on the piece of white paper.

When I'm done, just about to turn away, he opens his mouth. "I heard about Amy," he says.

I freeze, unable to respond.

"I read the article in the *Gazette*," he says. A smirk tugs at the corners of his lips.

And I am sick. I am so sick at this new, sadistic Peter. At the way that he's fucking gloating over Amy's death.

How can he have forgotten how beautiful she was?

My hands curl into fists. I want to hit him, even though, shit, what was I expecting from this boy?

"I heard," he says, tone mild, as if he's talking about the weather or something, "that she jumped off your roof. Does it suck knowing that maybe, just maybe, if you didn't have a three-story house, she wouldn't be dead?"

And it's at this exact moment that Tristan shows up. It is these words that he catches, and he looks at me with all this sympathy. And even though I don't want to see that look on his face, that look of pity, I can't do anything. Can't say anything. Because I'm afraid I'm going to fucking explode. So I just stand there trembling. Trembling, and wondering how the fuck Peter Paton can say this to me.

Wondering when he started his love affair with cruelty.

"Man," Tristan says when it becomes clear that I'm not going to speak. "What is your problem? That's just not cool."

Breathing, it's a fucking battle right now. So I do the only thing I can think of to center myself: I smash my fist into the desk. Pain shoots through my wrist, hot and cold. Pins and needles. Thorns and briars. Pain burns away my fragility, stops me from trembling.

"What are you *doing*?" Peter stumbles back.

He's looking at me like I'm a psychopath. And I don't have an answer to his question that won't confirm that I am one. So I stay silent. We both stay silent and keep staring at each other. Neither of us wants to seem too afraid to meet the other's eyes. But the truth is, I'm scared shitless.

I'm scared shitless, because I fucking did this. Or at least I partially did this. Me and Amy, and everyone else who stood by and watched us say the things we said to this boy. Mark and Petal. The entire student body of Sherwood High.

"It's sad," I say eventually.

The silence splinters all around us.

"What's sad?" Peter says. And his voice is so sharp that it cuts into me.

It's sad that Amy's parents haunted her out of her skin. And then Amy haunted Peter out of his skin.

"You are so much like her now." I'm close to tears. "You don't know it," I say, "but you're just like Amy."

"Don't compare me—"

But I head outside before he can put up a meaningless defense.

Casey sits alone as usual, a piece of red chalk jammed between her fingers. She's scribbling blood-colored dust over the dull gray concrete.

When she sees me, she smiles.

"Hi," I say.

"Hi."

I sit down next to her, ignoring all the other children racing around the play equipment, buzzing with energy. Tristan will be with them soon, and I'm pretty sure that Heather doesn't want me dealing with any of these kids.

Except for Casey, apparently.

I look at her. Her head's bowed, with curtains of mousy brown hair blocking her face from view. But words are trickling from her mouth, and I can hear them. "What do you think my life's really going to be like?" she says without looking up at me.

I want to sing to her. Want to sing, "*Que sera, sera,* whatever will be, will be."

But I'm not cruel enough to do it.

"Why do you want to know?" I ask.

She shrugs. Her shoulders are tiny. God. She's tiny.

Ten years old.

"Just do."

Ten years old and wrapped in weariness from head to toe. I don't know what's wrong with Casey. But I know *something's* wrong.

"Okay," I say. I'm not sure how to answer, though. I don't know how to unravel her life's story for her. I don't even feel in control of my own life's story most of the time. I feel as if I've been telling it all wrong.

"Okay," I repeat. I'm not sure where to begin.

"My story is just okay?" Her words are biting, each of them a tiny piece of disappointment. "What does that mean?"

I clear my throat, willing an answer to float into my brain. "It means that you're going to be okay. In the end, we're all okay."

My finger dances through dusty gravel. I draw swirls, swirls, swirls.

I'm not even sure if I believe what I just said.

Because Amy was my best friend, and in the end she wasn't okay. She had her moments where she floated up high—breaking into supermarkets, dancing in fountains, mooning the local pastor—but in the end she hit the ground. In the end she wasn't okay. She was all wrong, crossed out, a stain of a body sprawled among the weeds in my garden.

"Are you sure?" Casey says.

"Yes," I say. "I'm sure."

Because I want to believe this.

I want to believe that I'm going to be okay. That we're all going to be okay.

But I don't and we won't and I just can't do this. Can't lie to this poor kid so badly, because she was right the other day when she said that, in stories, the ending is always too happy. I open my mouth. "Casey," I begin, but then someone else speaks. Cuts me off.

"What have you done?"

Heather's got her hands on her hips, pressing today's floral blouse into the curves of her body. Her face is red, red, red; and her lips are pursed. Bloodless.

I shrug and get to my feet, ready for a showdown. Or a meltdown. "I don't have a clue. Why don't you tell me?"

Doubtless this has something to do with Peter.

"How dare you," she breathes. "How dare you waltz

in here and tell my son that he's like *that girl?*"

I close my eyes.

That girl.

Amy. My best friend.

My bitch of a best friend who is *dead*.

I'm too tired to play nice or to keep up my wholesome act. "Because," I say. "Because it's the truth."

She leans in, way too close. "No," she says. "It isn't. My son is nothing like your friend. Like you."

She spits out *you*. As if being compared to me is worse than being compared to a fucking ax-murderer. As if I'm a serial killer-arsonist-whore.

I can't speak, can't say anything to show her that she's wrong.

But then Casey wraps her chubby, warm fingers around my knee.

It's as if Casey's grounding me, telling me that I'm not that bad. I've been stupid, and I've made mistakes; but I'm not that bad. I have love and hate and anger and sorrow and pain in this body, just like anybody and everybody else. Just like Heather and her son.

I keep my head high, hold my ground. Because I may not be the best person, but I'm not the worst, either. I tell Heather the truth. "He's becoming exactly like us," I say, "whether you like it or not."

She steps back because she can hear in my voice that

I'm telling the truth. Because she really doesn't want me to be telling the truth.

"How could—"

"We broke him," I say. "He's becoming like us because we broke him."

Her nostrils flare. "Get out! I don't need you here. I don't want you here. Just get out. Get the fuck out."

I want to argue with her. I want to stand there and tell her that I'm not poison, that I'm a worthy human being. But the words would taste false. Because to her, I'm always going to be the girl who killed her son's spirit. To her, I really will always be poison, even though I'm trying to change. Even though I think I *have* changed since what happened with Peter.

So instead of pulling out defensive words, I step around her and walk toward the playroom. Toward the exit. Light streams through the glass doors, the glass windows.

We're all just people in glass houses.

Peter's still standing behind the registration desk when I come inside. I pause, stare at him. He can feel my gaze—I know because of the way he starts coughing. He shuffles and reshuffles the papers in front of him way too many times.

And then I'm heading back over to him. I'm heading back over to him because I have something to say. Because I don't want the ghost of the girl I used to be to haunt me anymore.

I prop my elbows up on the blue counter. "Hey," I say.

He edges back, away from me. "Shouldn't you be gone?"

"Probably. Your mom's going to kill me if she sees me still here."

"But she can't see you from outside," he says, biting his lip. He looks so freaked-out.

I resist the temptation to roll my eyes. "Relax," I say. "I'm not going to bite you."

He stares at the table. Shuffles the papers. Again and again. Cough. Eventually, he looks up at me, his face all hard lines. Cut glass. "What the fuck do you want from me?"

"I just wanted to say . . ." Pause. I suck in a deep breath. Once I say this there's no going back, no finding that old Ella with all the careless words and apathy. Once I say this I'll no longer have any fucking clue about who I am.

I say it, anyway.

"I'm sorry."

Chapter Twenty-two

I HAVE NOWHERE TO GO. SO I'M SITTING RIGHT OUTSIDE the center. Sitting beneath an oak tree on a carpet of smashed autumn leaves. Wind whips up and down the street. I bow my head against it, wondering what the fuck I'm still doing here.

But I know.

I'm waiting for Tristan in some ways. Waiting and waiting and waiting because he's promised to show me what Amy felt like, and no one else has been able to make me that promise.

I'm also waiting for the end of time. Infinity. Forever. Because I can't leave this place, can't leave Sherwood, even though I want to more than anything.

People think that only small towns are stifling, only small-town life slings nooses around people's necks and leaves them to hang. Sherwood isn't a small town—Sherwood is big and sprawling and packed with stately houses. And still, I've always wanted to escape.

I'm convinced I've been singing the Big Town Blues since the day I was born. And I'm convinced that Amy was, too.

But she's dead and gone now and I'm here, squished against rotting autumn leaves on a deserted road. Still. Life is as still as death today.

I bury my head in my hands. *Don'tthinkdon'tthinkdon't think*—

Three days before Amy jumped, we went back to the park. To the jungle park where we used to get so tangled up when we were young. We played hide-and-seek again. And we raised a bottle of vodka. We drank to each other's health. We laughed. We danced. We pretended to be fairies just like when we were five.

And after the energy fizzled from us—escaped our bodies through our toes and our heads, gusted out of our open, laughing mouths—we lay down on the ground and stared up at the sky. That day, that day when we were dreaming, I was so sure I could snatch a cloud out of the sky, pop it into my mouth, and taste cotton candy. Taste hope.

There were branches above us with leaves dripping down, glowing golden in the light. The earth was soft beneath us.

We smiled at the world that day. The world was infectious that day.

"Ella," Amy said. "You've got to help me find the horizon before we go to college together."

"The horizon? Are you serious?"

"Yeah! We'll steal Cherry Bomb—grand theft auto, you *know* you want to—and we'll just drive until we slam into it. Or until everything feels like sun around us."

"You're so weird right now. Been messing with your boyfriend's stash?"

"Nah. I just want his car and his body, not his drugs."

She was lying.

That was two days before she died, two days before my party. Two. Fucking. Days. She couldn't have had such a radical change of mind in two days, could she?

I don't get it.

I just don't.

Why did she tell me all that if she was going to die? Why did she tell me that we'd be going on some crazy road trip to the horizon together, that we'd be going to college together, if she was going to leave me alone in Sherwood?

Part of me can't help but wonder whether, maybe, she wanted to reach the horizon so she could see if there was anything on the other side.

I feel like an unnecessary piece of garbage dumped at the airport.

It doesn't help that the center's about to close and the parents are showing up in their SUVs and sports cars and Hondas. They look down at me. And then the kids start to come out of the center, and they look down at me, too. Down, down, down their noses.

They can see her. The ghost of the girl I used to be, who will haunt me forever. And Amy. Sometimes I think Amy's death is as visible on us—me and Mark and Pet—as our clothes, our hair, our fuck-off stares.

Today, I don't, can't shoot anyone with my glare. Instead, I stare through strands of brittle black hair at the concrete, at the bruised autumn leaves.

The kids—Nike, Reebok, Nike, Converse, Converse— get swallowed up inside the cars, which cruise away down the street. The engines drone off into the distance.

And then the sound dies and I'm alone again.

Waiting for Tristan.

Where is he?

I turn my head looking for him. Searching him out. But all I can see are sapling trees and the twigs of the oak crisscrossing overhead, brown bars preventing me from leaping into the gray sky. It takes me a moment to realize that there's actually another person out here, too.

Casey.

She's sitting right in front of the entrance to the center,

leaning against the base of a streetlight. Her legs kick across the now-smudged lines of a hopscotch game, the edge of an electric blue *3* curling out from beneath her feet.

I wave when I catch her eye. Because this is what friendly, nonbitchy people do. They wave at ten-year-olds who seem as if the world has washed over them, washed into them, washed them out.

She waves back. Tugs at her hair. Even at this distance I can see that something's making her uncomfortable. And that's when I notice the car crawling toward the center. Battered. A blue version of Cherry Bomb. Blueberry Bomb. The driver's got the window rolled down, and rock music and cigarette smoke float out the window.

There's a voice crawling out the window, too. "Casey, get in the car."

And I'm on my feet, not sure why, not sure what I'm going to do. There's a part of me that's dying inside for Casey, because the woman in the car—her mom I'm guessing—doesn't care enough about her to put out the fucking cigarette. But it's more than that. It's the tone of her mother's voice.

Shrapnel to my ears.

Casey stands, drags her feet to the car.

The woman blows out a huge plume of smoke. "Hurry up."

Casey doesn't respond. She opens the car door, gets inside. Her face is blank. Slack jaw, empty eyes.

Blueberry Bomb begins to move. I look up as it goes past me, and Casey's staring straight at me. "Fuck," she mouths, grinning. Like this is her secret rebellion or something.

Kid's got premature teen spirit.

Wheels turning, burning by, and then they're gone, speeding up the street way too fast.

And now I know *for sure* that something's up with Casey. That she is well on her way to becoming exactly like my best friend, the girl who swears too much, parties too hard, drives too fast, drinks too much, and eats too little.

When you're that age and you've got someone like that woman in the car, it's so hard to know what to be.

I'm about to sit back down when I see Tristan emerging from the center.

"Hey," he says, walking over to me. "I didn't think you'd wait for me."

Why not? Why not, when he's offering to show me what Amy felt, what Amy thought? That's all I want, and he's offering it to me.

"Anyway, sorry I'm a bit late. I was busy punching out that Peter guy for ratting on you to Heather."

"Really?"

He may just have stolen my position as the worst volunteer.

"No, not *really*." His eyebrows are about to soar off into the sky, he's so shocked that I believe him. "Do I look like the kind of guy who randomly punches people?"

I remember the *thwack* his fist made when it collided with Mark's cheekbone.

I want to tell him that, yeah, he does. But he seems so incredulous. I'm pretty sure that's not the answer he's expecting.

I shift. Weight on my left foot, weight on my right. And then I shift again, because I still don't know what to say. Because he's got explosive hair, and he's dressed in black and gray and blue, and he smells like fucking gunpowder.

What does he want me to say?

"Well—"

He runs a hand through his hair. "Okay. Don't answer that question. Let's just go."

"Where?" I say. "Ghost Town?"

He seemed pretty interested in it on Saturday, but he didn't actually say that we'd be going there.

"You don't find out until you get there. Don't be a

curious bitch." He throws my words back at me, a tiny smirk edging the corners of his lips.

God. I hope this doesn't end with him tossing me off a bridge.

Chapter Twenty-three

I NEED THE GNOME. THIS IS THE ONLY THOUGHT SAND-wiched inside my skull as I walk with Tristan.

We're walking beside the jungle path of my childhood. Memories threaten to leap out of the trees and drag me into the shadowy undergrowth.

Tramp. Tramp. Tramp. Our footsteps reverberate off the concrete, the sound zinging into the sky. Suddenly, he breaks off the path, heads into the jungle. I hesitate before following him.

Weeds underfoot, branches overhead. I can barely make out the sky. I can barely resist the temptation to open my mouth and call, *Amy, come out, come out, wherever you are!*

It's been more than a month since she died, and it still feels as if I haven't processed her death. I still forget that she's gone, that I can't speak to her.

My breathing gets heavier.

Silence sits between us for too long, grows uncomfortable. We shift within it. Our footsteps become clipped. More clipped. The clipped-fucking-est.

"Where are we going?"

"Do you *want* me to blindfold you?"

"Fuck you," I mumble before I can think it through.

Guilt stabs through my stomach. *Bitch.* It's not as easy a personality type to shake as I thought it would be. Careless words seem to fall out of my mouth more easily than breaths.

Tristan's warm, hazel eyes go dull for a second. And then, nice guy that he is, he turns my rudeness into a joke. "Oh, are we up for the orgies part then?"

"Yeah, we just need to find some other participants. Two people do not an orgy make, honey."

"Honey?"

"It's a part of my vocabulary," I say. "Don't take it too seriously."

He holds his hand to his chest. As if I've shot him. "So wounded, Ella. So wounded."

"And I don't give a shit."

"How about two shits? Or three? Come on. Make me a lucky boy."

And I realize, slightly too late, that this ridiculous conversation has gotten me through the jungle park, gotten me through without too many dark imaginings, too many memories of Amy's sunlit brown hair swishing behind tree trunks.

We're heading toward the river. Over damp earth, as black as ashes. We're heading through a burned-out world toward the river.

Tristan says, "Do you want me to put you out of your misery?"

Yes. No. Maybe.

He's either going to tell me where he's going or reveal that he's a serial killer.

I don't think I care either way.

"Yeah, end my pain."

I say it sarcastically, but I mean it. God, I mean it. If someone could just take it. Take it all away.

The images of Amy's perfect, twisted limbs. The ache in my chest that's always there. The thoughts and questions that circle around me, circle behind me, loop about my neck. It's the thoughts and questions that push me. Off the top floors of barns, off bridges.

Tristan snatches a stick from the ground. He slices it through the white-gray sky so that it's pointing across the river. At the houses. The abandoned houses, all of them coming apart, unraveling. All of them sweet, rotting wood and pot smoke from the "rebellious" local kids who were too bored at home.

I imagine Amy's ghost rattling through loose planks inside one of those houses. Dark and dank and deathly.

"Ghost Town," he says. He drops the stick.

These houses, they're made of pieces of wood that you can tell were once logs. The planks have been roughed up; long slits slide down their faces. They all look totally washed-out and eroded. Once, twice, three times a year, according to my eighth-grade history class, this place used to flood. That's why it's abandoned.

I turn to Tristan. He stands beside me, hands thrust deep into pockets.

"So we stay in Ghost Town. To isolate ourselves?" I ask.

"Yeah, basically."

"Sounds like fun," I drawl. "But the local kids hang out here all the time. It's hardly the most isolated spot."

He makes a face. "Really? It's probably rat-infested and crawling with cockroaches."

I almost retch but manage to stop myself just in time. The thought of insects whispering like ghostly leaves over my bare skin sickens me. The thought of squeaking rats.

He catches my expression and rolls his eyes. "Jesus. You can handle almost killing yourself every day but mention a few cockroaches . . . Besides, it's a little late for the kiddies to be out."

It's only six o'clock, but he's right—the younger kids have probably left by now. I wonder how long Tristan intends for us to stay here. Whether there's a chance of me missing my eleven-o'clock curfew. Whether there's a chance of Mom actually noticing.

And suddenly I feel cold all over. Because, really, who do I have? Not Dad, who drove away from me the other night. Not Mark and Pet, who can't even look at me. My mother, surprisingly, is the one person in my life who's actually trying to help; but she's so bad at it that I just don't know anymore. I don't know whether I have anyone.

"I still don't understand what the point of this is," I say.

His shoulders slope up, become hillcrests before they dip back down. "It's my best guess as to what suicidal people actually feel like: isolated, alone, frustrated. And if you get freaked out enough, you can maybe get some of your memories back."

He's tucked the piece-of-hay thought he stole from me yesterday behind his ear. I reach over and recapture it, ignoring the way he flinches. We haven't known each other long; it's reasonable that he's uncomfortable with me getting that close.

I roll the hay between my fingers, roll my thoughts around my brain. He's right. There's no way around it.

"Don't forget tunnel vision. You have to be alone, and you have to have tunnel vision," I say.

"Maybe we should look this up or something?"

"Later. Let's go be alone."

His shoulders rise and fall again. He looks like something out of a cartoon when he does that, what with his carrottopped hair. "I thought we could ease into it. We could stay together for the first hour or so and then split up?"

My teeth grind into each other. "I don't need you to ease me into it. I'm not that frightened of cockroaches."

Yes, yes, I am. If we ever do this again, I'm bringing one of those spray insect killer things.

Tristan barely blinks. He looks at the ground. "Right," he says. "Thing is, I'm kind of afraid of the dark. So it's not about you."

There's an accusation laced through those words. He's telling me not to think everything's about me. Thanks, Tristan.

"Okay," I say, feeling winded.

It hurts because he's goddamn right. I could have stopped her—maybe not that night, maybe not the week before or the month before. But years ago, ninth grade when she started losing weight. I could have taken her to McDonald's and sat her down and bought her a Big Mac and said, "It's cool. You can eat processed shit once in a while because it feels good."

We could have laughed and thrown fries at each other. I could have recommended her to my mother's therapist or something.

I could have. But I didn't.

"You okay?"

Tristan's looking at me, and the shadows of the night are crisscrossing his face so I can barely make out his features. I like it this way, because I can imagine for a second that he's Mark, Petal, Amy.

"I'm fine," I say.

And then he starts grinning his head off. And even in the dark I can see his white teeth, the moonlight bouncing off them. A manically grinning grenade and I are about to walk into an abandoned house teeming with cockroaches. Wonderful.

Just. Fucking. Wonderful.

I think I preferred jumping off shit.

We decide on the house that's the most dilapidated looking. Or, at least, I decide on it.

He doesn't seem too happy. "You know," he says as we traipse up the front steps, "there are probably more cockroaches in this one."

"Shut up, Tristan." My shoe hits the wood and crunches into something. I scream, but the sound thuds into the wooden front door and gets lost in the house. When I lift my foot, it's not a cockroach or a rat.

It's a fucking bag of chips.

Tristan's cracking up. He's nearly falling off the stairs, and right now I could push him.

I don't even bother glaring at him. "Let's go inside. Maybe your hair can be a torch or something."

He laughs. "Hey, don't bring my hair into it."

I push at the door, but it's jammed. Apparently, the neighborhood kids have also noticed that this is the most dilapidated house around. Apparently, no one wants to hang out here, in this particular house, except me.

The isolation is already creeping into my bones.

And I want it to creep farther. I want it to creep so far that it reawakens my memories.

So I step back and kick at the door. It shudders, but it's made of sturdier stuff than I thought and doesn't give way. Dirt shakes itself from the deep wrinkles that score the wood.

"Nice. Try and break down the door, Ella. Good luck. Why don't we just go through the window?" Tristan jabs his finger.

My gaze slides to the side of the house. The window is an opportunity in this rotten wall of wood. I jump off the side of the stairs—not quite high enough to feel like a Pick Me Up. But high enough that I laugh when I land.

High enough that I feel giddy.

Tristan hauls his butt down the stairs, step by step by

step. He doesn't even take them two at a time. It's as if he's trying to show me the proper way of doing things. Like he thinks I don't know how to walk down a freaking staircase.

But it's hard to be pissed at him when I feel so heady with pain shooting up from my ankles. I'm submerged in knee-high grass. It swishes and sways against my calves, breezing across my skin as I wade through it to the window. The frame is empty except for a few jagged pieces of glass.

I punch them out. They topple into the grass at my feet, and Tristan kicks them away into the darkness.

"Watch it," he says. "Don't cut yourself."

"I wasn't intending to."

I wrap my fingers around the sharp metal frame of the open window. Rust flakes off it and falls down my arm like dried blood. I shudder. This is so disgusting. If I were one of those girls who cared about her nails, I wouldn't do this.

"Are you going or what?"

I flip Tristan off with my free hand. Flipping each other off is going to become a tradition with the two of us, I can tell.

"I'm going." I stop giving him the finger and swing my other hand up, curl my fingers over the rotting wood wall. Heave-ho. Like a sailor. I haul myself halfway up. My feet scrabble against the wall. My arms burn. The wood splinters.

I scramble, shinny up the wall, and fall over the ledge. Rotting wood splinters beneath my fingers, crashes onto the floor with my body.

"Oof."

The rancid, sweet-and-sour smell of rotted wood hits my nostrils. This is the smell of death. This house hasn't been stepped in for how long now, ten years? Twenty?

"Are you okay?" Tristan has the gall to sound concerned.

"I'm giving you the finger again."

But I'm shivering against the floor and feeling the grime beneath my fingers. Feeling the pain in my stomach where it smashed into the wood.

This is the beginning of Isolation Stage One, and it is cold and wet, made of echoes and silence.

Until Tristan decides to follow me into the dark.

To my relief, my grenade companion is not graceful, either. The advantage of being a whole head taller than me doesn't help him. He looks like he's constipated as he tugs himself through the window.

Wood splintering, breaking.

We're breaking this abandoned house down. This abandoned house is breaking us down.

My mouth tastes as foul as the smell in this house. I can't see Tristan's face, but I can tell from the way he's singing "Shit. Fuck. Crap" again and again, words like a dog chasing its own tail, that he's not exactly enjoying this, either.

Isolation sucks.

And we're not even totally isolated.

The window is still open. A square of dull moonlight carves a path through the room, and dust motes dance in the beautiful light. Like Amy's beauty, I think. Dancing, whispers and smiles on the surface. But the inside must have been like this: black and hollow. Eaten away by termites and dust.

When she was tangled in my weeds in front of the gnome, her lungs might have collapsed like this house's staircase. Her heart might have splintered like this wood. I'll never know what happened to Amy physically. But emotionally?

I reach out and shut the window. *Click*.

As if reading each other's minds, Tristan and I both turn our backs on the window and face the dark.

Breathe. Breathe. Breathe.

Chapter Twenty-four

WE ARE CURLED AGAINST THE WOOD LIKE COMMAS.

Something creeps over my sneaker, and I shake my foot. The scream that tears from my mouth is swallowed by the hands I have wrapped around my head. I lift my head from my hands, swallow away the dryness in my mouth. Tears prick the backs of my eyes like needles.

It doesn't matter. It's dark. He can't see me.

I say, "Since when have we been friends, anyway?"

I feel his eyes boring through the stench of sweet-and-sour rot. Focused on the blurry shape of my face in the darkness. "We're friends?" Soft voice. Sweet voice. It only adds to the general feeling of sweet sickness in this room.

I'm shivering and I'm shivering and I'm shivering, and he must be able to hear me in the dark or something. Because he's there suddenly, and his arms are around me and he's warm and the air is cold. I should twist away. I should tell him to fuck off. I should do *something* to show that I'm okay and that I don't need his help.

But it's like I've already decomposed. I'm crashing into his shirt. I'm crying into the soft material, letting my tears soak him.

Where were you? When Amy died? Ella?

Everyone asks me all the time.

I don't know what to say. I can never answer their questions.

Tristan doesn't move. Just lets me cry into his shoulder with his hands limply at his sides. It's only when I start to shift, to move that his hand touches my back, and he pats me awkwardly. "It's okay, Ella," he says, his voice strangled. "Maybe this wasn't a good idea."

The tears are hot, sliding down my cheeks. I brush them away quickly. "No! We're doing this."

I'm inside Amy's mind. This is where I want to be. This is where I want to stay. This is what I need to understand.

Heavy breaths, colliding like cars crashing on a dark winter's night.

His fingers, combing through his hair. Raspy laugh.

"Fuck," I repeat, "since when were we friends, anyway?"

I can feel his face against my shoulder. He smiles into

my hair, and it's like sunshine in the dark. "Since I decided to be a dumb shit," he replies, "and become insanely into friendships with bitchy, hot girls."

I don't bother to be self-deprecating. If he wants to call me hot, that's his prerogative. I detach myself from his shirt, though. "So—"

"So we're totally alone in the dark," he says.

"Dear lord. How the hell do I know you're not some pervert?"

"Because I wouldn't be so up-front about wanting to get into your pants if I were."

I can hear the laugh sitting beneath his voice. It tastes like popcorn and the sky. Isolation isn't working, because Tristan is here, and he shouldn't be here. I'm supposed to be alone, the dark weighing in on me, suffocating me.

"We have to shut up," I say. "You have to shut up. You can't speak—" I swallow. "We have to be alone."

"Well," he mutters, "that was a convenient change of topic."

I stifle a laugh and turn my back on him, pretend he's not there. His breathing still crashes around me. Waves against the shore. He wants to speak; I know he wants to speak. Because I do, too. Words leap to my lips every ten seconds.

Do you miss your brother?

Is it my fault? Do you ever feel like it was your fault?

And then there are more innocuous things:

What's your favorite song? What do you think could break this silence?

Who would you rather do? Stalin or Hitler? It's Petal's party question.

I force these questions to ride the slippery slope back into my mind.

I have no idea how long we sit there, but it must be a long time. Because eventually my legs feel like stone, and I can't feel my body. The silence isn't only around me; it's *in* me. Flowing through my blood. Icing up my arteries. Freezing my heart.

I become blue, blue, blue. So this is what it's like to be isolated. This is how Amy felt.

It's an effort of will to stand here, full of silent thought, and keep myself upright. It's an effort of sheer fucking will.

And eventually, I break. I slide to the floor, and I'm shivering. I'm going into panic-attack mode. Crap.

The ice turns to fire in my limbs. Kick, kick, kick. The dirty wooden floor of the house gives way beneath me. My legs curl into my chest. My head collapses into my chest. Teeth, chattering uncontrollably, collide with my lips. Blood.

Blood spills.

Tristan falls to the floor, falls through the dark to sit beside me. His knees hit the battered, bruised wood. He whispers, "Shit, this was a bad idea," faintly in the background. But I'm already falling into the dark chasm that is my mind. I'm already going, going, gone.

The bottle smashes on my fence. "Fuck you, fuck you, fuck you, Aaron!" I singsong at the boy who broke it. He grins, shakes a lock of hair into his eyes. He thinks he's a cute drunk.

He's wrong.

"Get him the fuck outta here," I snarl at his friends.

They surround Aaron, ferry him down the side passage of my house, out of my backyard and onto the street. They slowly disappear. One of them pauses beneath the streetlight to salute me. I give him the finger, and drunken laughter floats back to me.

"Fuck you, too, Ella. See you tomorrow."

There comes a point when you're so bitchy all the time that no one gives a damn anymore. But hating everyone is exhausting, exhausting, exhausting. And Amy's with me, and she's drunk as fuck and trying to lick the shards of glass.

I pick her up off the grass. She heaves in my arms, and vomit splatters the ground. "What happened to not drinking, huh, Ames?"

She slurs something I can't even hear. Doof-doof-doof, *the bass beat in the house thumps.*

"Do you want to crash in my bedroom?"

She sounds as if she's choking, and she vomits again. Looks up at me with the baleful eyes of a drunk. Oh, right. Mark and Pet were making out in front of my parents' bedroom. Amy's best friend and boyfriend of the past four years.

"Okay, well, let's crash here then."

I tug on Amy's hand, tug her out to a spot that's free of glass shards and vomit. She flops down first, and I follow. The grass is a soft tickle, and the ground beneath it is even softer. This is the best bed ever. The stars are out, and the moon is out.

In my peripheral vision the shards of the bottle pick up the moonlight. Amy is slurring on my other side, and I can't hear what she's saying.

"Speak up, Ames."

The bass beat. God, my head hurts. I can't believe I'm still sober enough to give a shit about any of this. I had so much to drink during that stupid game, but I'm still not under. Not quite yet. I'm tempted to grab a beer just so Amy and I can be drunk and miserable together.

"You know," Amy says, her voice thick. But she doesn't bother to pursue her thought. Instead, she plucks a piece of grass and blows her nose with it. I laugh at her, and she joins in, tentatively at first, then hysterically.

It's the hysteria that tells me this moment can't go on being peaceful forever. That this moment is going to shatter, like the shards of whiskey bottle in the moonlight.

It's going to fucking explode.

"You know," Amy repeats. Whiskey-whisper. How drunk is she? What the fuck is she going to say? And will it be true, or will it

just be a product of her blood-alcohol level? There's no way for me to know.

"Mark and Pet together so doesn't surprise me."

Her hand lashes out, bumbles in the dark, and finds my stomach.

"It surprised me."

She turns onto her side so she's facing me instead of the moon and then she says, "But you know, Ella."

I look at her and she looks at me, and I wish that she'd just stop saying "you know." I wish she'd stop beating around the bush and tell me what she's going on about.

Suddenly, she's so close and her foul breath is colliding with my cheek. "I've never really loved Mark. He was always just the next best. The next best, I could get because——" Her laugh floats like oil through the thick midnight air.

She's taking her time. It feels mysterious; and even with the rap music eating my ear off, I want to shout. It's just what you do at midnight.

But then Amy's speaking. And I have to be attentive because she looks like she's going to vomit again. And she does, only this time she word-vomits. "I never wanted Mark. I wanted——" She's crying now, tears crawling down her cheeks like snails. "I wanted you."

"Oh, ha-ha, very funny," I say.

But we're still looking at each other, and she's so fucking close. "Amy?" I say, because she doesn't look like she's joking. But god, I don't know whether this is Amy speaking or drunk-Amy speaking or what.

And whoever it is, it doesn't matter. Because I. Do. Not. Know. How. To. Handle. This.

"You're kidding, right?"

But she doesn't say right, and the matter doesn't blow over. Instead, the moment blows up. She leans over and starts to kiss me. She tastes of alcohol. And god, it's clumsy. I try to concentrate on the glass sparkling in the grass rather than the whiskey lips pressing against mine.

I've kissed girls before, on dares and whatnot, so I'm thinking that I can handle it.

But then she starts trying to slip me the tongue, and my head is exploding like a supernova. White noise rings, rings, rings in my head. What. Is. She. Doing? Where does this leave our friendship? She's drunk. She'll regret this tomorrow morning.

She's my best friend; I don't want to upset her. But I can't let her do this.

I reach out and put a hand against her chest. I push her, and she falls away easily.

"Amy?" I say.

She touches her lips. They tremble beneath her fingers. "Oh god," she whispers. "Oh god. What have I done?" She's still slurring. "You don't . . . you're not. You don't swing that way." She makes a ridiculous swishing movement with her hips, cutting through the grass. "You told me yourself, and you don't lie about shit like that, do you?"

"No," I answer. I don't know what else to say. And I don't know

who to be angry with anymore. Because if Mark is fooling around behind Amy's back but Amy's never really been into Mark, then I don't know who's at fault.

God. Fuck morality.

All I know is that I love them both.

And then there's a click and a flash of silver light. Camera. I turn around, and Mark's standing there. Shit.

"Just getting some party shots," he says. "You and I cool, Amy?"

She vomits in response, and he just watches us for a second.

There's something weird in the way he twists his fingers through his purple ninja-tied style bandanna. How long, exactly, has he been standing there? I ask with my eyes, and he shakes his head.

Oh. Crap.

That can only mean that he's been standing there forever.

"Mark—" I say, but he's already gone. The door swings shut, and he disappears, gets lost in the sounds of the party.

Amy curls up beside me, crying as if she's absolutely broken.

And I am still. I am so still that I'm afraid the night is going to swallow me.

My chest is tight. My eyes are wide. I'm vaguely aware of my body quivering against the rotten wood. But my mind has become a blank. A black screen saver with one word, all in caps, ghosting across it in fluorescent green: *FUCK.*

What the fuck happened after Amy kissed me?

Oh god, I feel so sick, and I'm shaking and my teeth

are chattering. The sickness is in my bones, in my heart, in my mind, in my stomach. Bile at the back of my throat.

It won't go away. No matter how much I keep shaking. Tristan's fingers tear at my arms as he tries to uncurl me, to stretch me out so I can breathe. But my mind is still a roar of white noise with swear words running through it.

"Ellaellaellaellaella." My name on repeat, the words bleeding into one another. It's almost like I don't know who I am anymore. Because I can't fucking remember.

The trembling is starting to recede. I can feel the splinters that have hooked themselves into my skin. Sharp pieces of wood spiked through my palms, my knees. The pain clears my head.

"Ella?" Tristan laughs. "Oh, thank god."

Thank god for what? Does he not realize that I'm poison for him, for anyone? Amy died.

He's opened the window. Moonlight waltzes into the room, caressing me.

"Got some of your memory back?" he asks. His voice is like butter, falling in chunks through the moonbeams.

I nod. My teeth are still chattering, still clacking into each other and threatening to turn my mouth into a war zone. "T-h-errre was a cammm-er-ra."

"What?"

And that's when I realize what I have to do. I have to find the camera, find the pictures—please, god, don't let

Mark have erased them. Maybe then I'll know whether he took a shot of Amy kissing me. Maybe then I'll know when the last shot of vodka went down. And why Amy went down.

Chapter Twenty-five

*M*Y MOTHER'S WAITING FOR ME WHEN I GET HOME. AND as soon as I'm through the door, she starts to throw a fit. I'm shocked. Fucking shocked that she even realized I was gone.

"I called you fifteen times!" she yells at me. "Fifteen times. And your cell was in your room." She waves my tiny silver phone around in the air. "Jesus Christ, Ella. Why do I even buy these things for you?"

And I'm trying so, so hard to be better than myself right now. But I still can't help letting her know the truth. Because I don't know when I'll see her again, when she'll act as if she gives a shit about me again. If Dad could just drive away in the middle of the night, then Mom can certainly go back to her old, workaholic self.

"Because you're never around, and you think you can buy my love," I tell her.

She turns off the TV. Ooh, so this is serious then.

"That hurt," she says.

"Well, Mom, the years of neglect have kind of hurt, too."

"Neglect—"

"How many conversations have we had in the past year? Come on, I can count them on one hand. Most of them have happened this month."

She adjusts her suit, runs her tongue over her lips. "Look, Ella, I'm trying my best, but I'm so busy with work—"

"Exactly," I say. "So why don't you just leave me alone? I'm not complaining. Please, do me a favor and go back to not caring."

She shakes her head. "I can't. I can't do that. Not when I know that you're in some kind of trouble."

I raise my eyebrows. "Trouble?"

"Your best friend died—you're grieving, sweetheart—"

Amy's death flipped some switch in my mother. Some switch that made her actually want to mother me. Maybe adults aren't that different from teenagers. Maybe they look at us, and they think we're going to live forever, just like we do.

Until one of us dies and shatters the illusion.

"Ella," my mother says, "you need me."

But I don't. I haven't needed her since I was ten and she stopped talking to me.

And god, I want to cry. Because I should need her. I should need my mother. But it's been too long. It's been far too long, and I can't even listen to her saying these things anymore. It's like a stranger's professing her love for me.

It feels fucking weird.

So I head toward the stairs, toward my bedroom. All I want to do is slither between the sheets and pretend to sleep. And think about how I'm going to get my hands on Mark's camera.

"Ella, get back here," my mom practically shrieks. "I'm your *mother*."

"When you choose to be."

I start making my way up the staircase, taking them two at a time.

"Don't you dare walk away from me!"

"Why not? Dad sure did."

"Your father and I are getting a divorce," she says, even though I've still got my back turned to her. I'm nearly at the landing now. "I was going to tell you; I didn't want you to find out like this—" I've never heard my mother this inarticulate before. "You know it just wasn't working out between us—it hasn't been for years. But it's different with you. You're stuck with me for life."

I keep heading up the stairs.

When I've made it to the safe zone of the landing, I hide in the shadows and finally turn around to look at my mother.

She's standing between our two couches, staring at the room as if she doesn't know what to do with herself. She picks up a cushion, brings it to her chest.

A lump barges into my throat. Maybe I should head back downstairs. Maybe I should open up to her about everything, cry on her shoulder like she seems to want me to.

But I can't. It would be too weird to cry on the shoulder of a woman I barely speak to beyond *hello*s and *good-bye*s and *good morning*s.

But I hope that maybe this is a first step, a step closer to each other. Because right now, I can imagine wanting to cry on her shoulder one day. I can imagine choosing to be her daughter one day.

And I couldn't imagine that this morning.

I shut my door quietly and slip between the covers even though I know that this is just a show I put on for myself. Even though I know that I'll swing my way out the window, Tarzan style, and climb up onto the roof in an hour or so.

I think about the memory that snapped into my brain

when I was thrashing on the floor of that house in Ghost Town. And with the covers curled up all around me, the world totally shut out, I press my fingers to my lips.

I still can't believe that Amy kissed me.

Chapter Twenty-six

*W*E'RE STANDING IN FRONT OF YET ANOTHER WINDOW THIS morning. So many opportunities sliding into my life lately.

I look up. Slice of pie-blue sky. I look down. Loose soil beneath my feet.

Tristan stands next to me, whispering a constant stream of swear words because we should be at school right now. Not about to commit a felony.

I turn to him. "Hoist me up?"

He shakes his head. Once, twice, three times. "I—Ella. What are we doing?"

"Breaking and entering, obviously."

I'm aware that my attempt to play it cool probably just looks stupid. After all, yesterday I was twitching on the floor of an abandoned house.

He rolls his eyes. "Obviously. *Obviously.*"

"You're the one who said you wanted to 'help me' get over Amy, right?"

"I wasn't aware it involved breaking the law."

"Well, it does. Now help me up if I need it, okay?"

Mark's bedroom window is on the ground floor, but his yard's on a steep slope, so there's a bunch of concrete foundation underneath the house to make sure everything's level. Which means his window is something I can only *just* reach with my fingertips.

I remind myself that this is not weird. I've done this before, when Mark and Amy and I sneaked out to a concert in tenth grade, and he and Amy and I crashed at his house after. God knows, Amy and I didn't want to go home and face our parents.

And Mark's parents just didn't give a shit.

The soil slips a little beneath my feet, and I reach up, curling my fingers around the window ledge.

I catalog the differences between this time and last time.

Last time, it was night. Last time, Mark and Amy were laughing like maniacs. Last time, I had permission to enter.

This time, I'm breaking in because I don't trust my oldest friend. And, shit, I'm beginning to sound like those girls who have fights with their friends in the school bathrooms. They're always going on about "trust" and what it means, and it's like *blah blah* in my head when they speak.

I don't want to be like them, *blah*-ing on forever, so I

stop thinking and start pulling myself up. My feet scrape against the side of the house. I look down and see the peeling white paint dancing away beneath my feet, falling to the ground like snowflakes.

My feet continue to scrabble. I'm not getting anywhere. It feels as if I'm running on a treadmill, kicking out against the same square of white wall over and over again. I lunge a little, dig my nails into the wooden sill, and hiss, "Tristan!"

"Oh, right."

He moves to stand under me, and suddenly his hands are beneath my feet and he's lifting. My arms get a little breathing space. I keep one hand on the sill and fasten the fingers of the other around the latch at the side of Mark's window and pull. It slides open.

Now to deal with the screen. Mark put it in a few years back when his house was getting invaded by cockroaches and ants. Except, being the lazy idiot he is, he didn't do it properly. The screen isn't attached to anything; it's placed against the inside of the window, and there's a little bit of tape on the side—I'm not kidding, he used fucking tape—to make sure it doesn't fall off.

I remove the tape, and the screen falls onto my head. Guess I should have thought that through a little more. "Ouch," I say, rubbing my scalp as Tristan's soft laughter floats up to me.

I give him the finger.

"Enough with the theatrics, Ella. Come on; get inside before I drop you. I'm not that strong, you know."

I leave my finger up and count to sixty. He groans; but hey, I like my theatrics, and there's no way I'm giving them up for Grenade Boy.

"Ella, I'm not kidding. My arms are killing me right now."

"Look on the bright side; you're building up some biceps," I reply, my tone absolutely flat. But I can hear him breathing heavily and hard.

So over the window sill I go. Tumbling and scraping my stomach on the wood in the process. Beige carpet catches me, cradles me. Dust motes shoot up my nostrils, and I sneeze. Remember that this is Mark's room I'm breaking into. Mark, who doesn't understand the meaning of clean.

I get up and shake my head, looking down at what I landed on. A pair of boxers—which would be gross no matter what was on them, but shooting stars, seriously? It's like he's out-hippied himself. A plastic bag and a pair of jeans. Thank god I didn't land on his belt buckle. That would've hurt.

"You okay?" Tristan calls.

"Yeah, fine. Where d'you think he'd hide his camera?"

"Shouldn't we, you know, be a bit quieter? Could

be someone in the house." His voice is quieter, barely audible. As if he's remembered that he should be sensitive.

I almost snort. This is Mark's house. "No one's ever home. Trust me."

He really does snort.

I don't waste too much time thinking about Tristan, though. I have to find the camera. The one with the images of me and Amy on it.

I try under the bed first. My fingers swipe through cobwebs and boxers. Yeah, this is gross.

When I speak to Mark again, I'm going to lecture him on flinging his underwear around, while somehow avoiding the fact that I know he does this because I broke into his bedroom.

I should feel guilty, but I don't. He's the one who's been lying to me for more than a month.

"Found it?" Tristan yells.

I shake my head before realizing he can't see me. "No."

"Tried the closet?"

I cast a sidelong glance at Mark's closet. Then I cross over the floor, skipping around and over and onto Mark's possessions. At one point I step on a skateboard and nearly roll away until I'm horizontal. His room is a fucking health-and-safety hazard.

When I get to the closet, I reach out and trace my

fingers over the ebony wood, the shiny silver handle, the poster of some band from the seventies no one's ever heard of—Mark loves his nostalgia. He sees the seventies as some kind of paradise.

I swallow and turn the handle, wondering what I'll find inside. The camera? Or something else? They say people keep their skeletons in the closet. . . .

The door swings open, slow and creaky, like the soul of some ghost is rattling around in the wood. Turns out Mark doesn't keep skeletons in his closet. But he doesn't keep clothes in there, either. He keeps what looks like a whole bunch of journals.

Except when I flick open one of them, it's full of photos. Photo albums. Mark keeps hundreds of photo albums. I flip quickly through one of the books. Some photos are of us. Under blue skies with clouds that he's altered in Photoshop. They look like the inside of an egg-shell.

The angles of the shots are interesting—like the one of Amy taken from behind, where she plays on a swing set as if she's six instead of sixteen. Her long legs fly into the sky, and her dyed-auburn hair flutters away from her face like a kite. The sun kisses her; the trees and sky seem to exist only to frame her.

In the side margins, scrawled in Mark's untidy hand-writing, is one word: *Happiness.*

Other shots are of landscapes, of skies pressing their orange lips against the ground. Of birds flying in formation. Mark's draped one of his scarves over the camera lens, and I see the picture through black-and-white checks. His annotation tells me he thinks the arrow of birds is *pointing me in the right direction.*

He reads nature, the world, like a book. Constructs it with his lens.

I've always known that Mark liked to be the one taking photos at parties, but I didn't know he was *this* into it. How could I not have noticed that Mark's a photographer? I guess it's just like how I missed out on Amy being depressed. I need to pay more attention. Really, truly, open my eyes.

I scan the albums. Some red-bound, others blue or brown, one with a purple background and dancing green aliens. I could spend hours looking through the photographs. But I resist, because I need to find that fucking camera.

Mark's closet is pretty wide. I climb inside it. The albums swoosh out around me as I cut a path through them, scattering Mark's memories so that they're out of order. Instinct tells me to head for the corner of the closet.

First the left one: nothing but a blue-skyrocket-covered photo album.

Then the right one: something wrapped in a purple scarf.

I pick up the scarf. Mark's tried to force it into a nice square shape, but slices of paper jut out at odd angles, and I can feel the uneven planes of an object beneath the fabric.

I get out of the closet, sloshing my way through the albums. They fall into one another. Memories colliding like dominos.

I dump the package onto the bed. Untie the corners.

The cloth unfolds like the petals of a flower, and I realize the thin, angular slices jutting out of the fabric are photographs. Developed, waiting to be put into an album. They're facedown, white backs glistening in the sunshine.

The camera is next to them.

I didn't think my fingers could move that fast. The camera is in my hands. Pinched between thumb and forefinger. Shiny metal, sliding away beneath my skin, smudged with my sweat. My breaths drip from my mouth like sweat.

"Ella?"

Apparently, Tristan can hear me.

I don't bother replying.

I push every single button on the camera until it beeps to life. Hope is climbing the staircase of my esophagus.

Hope is sitting in my mouth. Hope is fucking asphyxiating me. But when I fumble buttery fingers around, attempting to find the history and see the photos, a message in bright red flashes across the screen:

INSERT MEMORY CARD.

Fuck. Mark.

He's taken the pictures out. The photos. The memories that are *mine*.

There's this shriek of laughter, and it takes a second for me to realize that it came from me. I stuff my fist into my mouth, bite my knuckles. I scream until they're bloody and raw. The hope that was strangling me dissolves into black ashes. Soot in my mouth.

My eyes find the pile of photos in front of me. I flip them over, and suddenly I feel so light that I could float away. My laugh is heady, spinning around me like a gauzy scarf.

Mark may be able to tell me lies with his sideways words and his sideways smile, but the camera never lies.

I've found them.

Pictures of that night.

I flip through them quickly. He's written on all of them, taken out his grief and anger with permanent marker running across the glossy, compacted colors. On one he's shredded our faces. On another he's written

FuckFuckfuckfuckfuckfuckfuckfuckwHOOP DEDOO.

With quick fingers, I find the photo I'm looking for: Amy and I, sitting in the grass. He's drawn wreaths of flowers around our heads, love hearts around our toes. We look like nymphs surrounded by a garden of booze.

Our lips pressed against each other's.

I drop the photograph, and it floats back onto the purple scarf. My fingers move to my heart, to my throat. He saw. *He saw.*

His feelings, in that moment, twist through me like a knife. Betrayal, envy, hatred.

"Ella?"

"Yeah—" I run my fingers through my hair. It slips and slides out from between my fingers, refusing to bend to my will. I tilt my head, blowing the hair that's in my face out of the way. It's when my head is at that weird angle that I catch the writing in tiny blue pen cut into the side of the photo.

Dents, more than writing. A watermark of sorts on the moment Amy shattered.

I bring the photo back to my eyes. Closer, closer, closer. And suddenly the dents aren't just dents. They're words that I still can't make any sense of: *THE VIDEO IS WORSE.*

What fucking video?

But my mind is already connecting the dots. It's going into overload.

I sink into my memory, crying quietly, because this time I don't *want* to know.

Chapter Twenty-seven

*B*ROKEN. *MY VISION IS BROKEN LIKE THE BOTTLE. ITS SHARDS
glitter in the moonlight; I can see the amber whiskey from where I'm
standing. I raise my arms above my head. Slippery tiles slide beneath
my feet. "Whoa-oh-oh!" My arms windmill.*

I'm standing on my roof.

*"Careful. You're drunk." Petal steadies me. She's drunk, too.
She's just better at being drunk than I am.*

"I'm not as drunk as Amy," I point out.

*Amy's sitting farther down the roof than the rest of us, muttering
to herself. Her drunken words spill into the purple night and land in
the weeds of my garden.*

*"Ella," she says, turning around. "Ella." She pats the tile
next to her, and there's a clattering noise as it begins to slide away.
Amy quickly slides it back into place and laughs. Laughs and
laughs.*

*Someone behind me laughs, too. I turn, and Mark's there.
He's holding a camera in his hands. "And this," he whispers in a*

*conspiratorial voice, "is why Ella's parents are going to murder her
when they get back from DC." He takes a step, and another few
tiles slide away, flicking through beams of moonlight before landing
in the garden.*

*"Yeah, well," Amy says. "I'm going to kill you for kissing Petal,
when I'm sober."*

*Not drunk enough to forget that, apparently. Her head lolls, and
slobber falls out of her mouth.*

*Mark peers around the camera, eyes flashing a warning as
alarming as the red lights on an ambulance. I shoot him a look.
"Don't," I mouth. "Not now."*

*"What are you saying, Ella? What are you hiding from me?"
Amy slips her toes over the edge of the roof and dangles them in the
crisp night air.*

*Mark goes off. He doesn't even take his face out from behind
the camera. "Oh, she's only telling me not to get pissed at you
for acting like a self-righteous bitch when I know you kissed Ella
barely twenty minutes ago." His words sting worse than the cold
night wind.*

Amy is stunned, even in her stupor.

*Pet looks from me to Amy and then back again. "Wh-what?"
she manages to say.*

*"You heard me," Mark roars. "Amy made out with Ella. Amy
fucking said that the only reason she was dating me was because
she couldn't have Ella. Ella's had her heart since forever, apparently."*

243

I bury my head in my hands. I want them to stop. I want them to stop. I want them to stop.

But the words are spewing out of Mark's mouth. "Fuck, Amy. Why the fuck couldn't you tell me that you're gay? That's what it is, isn't it?"

Amy's crying now. She can't look at him. And he's moving over the tiles. They slip away, slide away. Doof, doof, doof. *Beating into the grass in time with the rhythm of the music floating up from the party.*

Mark stands next to Amy, and now he's crying, too. He drops a hand onto her shoulder. "Why couldn't you tell me?" he demands. "I would have loved you, anyway. Best friend, girlfriend, it wouldn't have fucking mattered. Why did you have to lie?"

I want her to say that she did love him. That she did fall in love with him once upon a time during those ninth-grade days when we were into ice-cream parlors more than drinking parties. I want her to say that she can love me and she can love Mark, because she's bisexual or something. Because then it wouldn't matter that she's always pretended to be straight.

None of us cares about her sexuality. None of us give a flying fuck.

But she thought we would.

I close my eyes. Midnight dew kisses the lids.

Amy speaks. "Because, Mark. Because I was a kid and I was confused and I didn't know what I was feeling. And I fucking hated it, you know? I fucking hated all of it. My parents kept on telling me I would turn into a guy if I kept getting fat like I did——"

In that moment I want to kill Amy's parents. I want to kill them for the subtle way their eyes would narrow when they looked over Amy's figure. The way they'd linger on her belly if they saw even the slightest bit of fat. Amy sucked in her stomach around her parents. She walked like she had a stick up her ass, like she was afraid of breaking whatever peace she'd managed to broker with them.

"My hormones would change and all——" She chokes. Tears flow past her lips and into her mouth, and she swallows. "So I thought, I thought that when I got thin——things would change. Or something. You were going to change me, Mark. You were going to save me."

His head droops; his curls droop. If I could see his face, I bet even his dimples would be drooping; but he's turned away. Shoulders heaving. Because he can't be her savior; he can't. And that's when it hits me: She went for him because she wanted me. I was supposed to be her savior.

It makes me feel like a bitter sin, sitting on mold-covered tiles.

"Please," Amy says. "Please, forgive me. . . . I, you were—— You were so beautiful."

Her sobs choke, choke, choke everything out of my world. For a second that's the only sound. The stars and moon disappear and the tiles beneath my feet vanish and I'm just floating and that sound is knifing into my back. Pure pain.

When the sound fades, Amy is standing, teetering on the edge of *my rooftop and Mark has taken a few steps back. His face is ghastly, paler than even the moonlight as he stares at her. "No, Amy." He shakes his head. "Don't."*

"It isn't worth it," Petal calls. "Whatever it is, whatever you've lost, it isn't worth your life."

But I've seen that look on Amy's face many times before. The way her jaw clenches, the way she looks at the world through lidded eyes. It was the same look she gave us just before we broke into a convenience store at three in the morning. The same look she had on her face when she kissed me.

Talking isn't going to stop her. Action might.

I get up and slip-slide over the tiles to where Amy's standing. I lace her fingers through mine, handcuffing her to the roof. There's no way she's going anywhere without me now. "Sit down, Amy," I say. "Sit down."

I make my voice harder than steel, make my determination match hers, and she starts to sit. She starts to sit. As I go down with her, I notice that the camera is still rolling. Perched higher than all of us on the roof, it takes in our every move.

I'm gasping. Sitting on the floor of Mark's bedroom. My fingers claw at his white sheets, scrabble through the photos. The sound of fingernails down a chalkboard as I scratch at their glossy surfaces and reveal the matte beneath. Scratched faces, scratched skin.

I can only scratch the surface of the past.

"Ella," Tristan's shouting now, pounding the side of

Mark's house. There's a crash and a clatter as he kicks something—probably one of those stupid metal buckets that Mark leaves outside to catch rainwater. Mark's into preserving things, into the self-sufficient lifestyle.

My tears come in floods, but I don't really feel them.

I'm crying because now I know what Mark meant by "the video is worse." I'm crying because now I know that the gnome wasn't the only one who saw Amy's last moments. I'm crying because I finally know where I was when Amy died: I was on the roof, watching her fall.

And now there's this suspicious voice in my head. . . .

What if it wasn't a suicide?

God. It may not have been a suicide.

What did we do? What did I see? What images did my mind photograph that night that were so painful they had to be shredded? Forgotten.

"ELLA!"

Tristan's roar is so loud that it's almost silent.

I seize onto his voice as if it's a rope swinging down to me in the abyss, an anchor. "Tristan." My voice is not my own. It's breathy. It slides up and down, plays a freaking piano scale.

"Tristan," I say again, my voice sounding slightly more normal. I gather the photos along with my thoughts, wrap them up securely in the purple scarf. "Tristan, stop kicking shit. I'm coming down now."

There may never be anyone home at Mark's. But I'm pretty sure if Tristan continues to trash everything in the garden, the neighbors are going to notice something's up.

Deep breath. Step. Deep breath. Step. Deep breath. Step.

I'm standing at Mark's window again. I pop my head out, breathe in the air, and then look down. Tristan's fuming. His head's going to explode if he gets any redder. And I didn't think hazel eyes could burn like forest fires—wild, angry flames—but Grenade Boy's proven me wrong.

"Fuck, Ella. What happened? Did you have another panic attack?"

I don't want to think this. I don't want to suspect this. But it's the only thing I can think of. My mouth dries out, and I swallow hard again and again. I close my eyes against the glare of the sun. But the world beneath my eyelids is orange, too fucking bright.

So I open my eyes. Face Tristan, face my own thoughts.

He looks so confused. The splinters are still breaking away beneath my nails. Everything is falling apart, breaking off. I won't be surprised if the window frame collapses when I climb through it in a second.

I speak the words that change this from a chase to find out what Amy felt before she died to a chase to find a killer: "I think one of us may have pushed her."

Chapter Twenty-eight

*W*IDE EYES. TRISTAN CAN'T KEEP HIS HANDS STILL. HE RUNS them through his hair. They fiddle with the buttons on his shirt. He accidentally undoes a few of them. Shit, his chest is toned underneath that shirt.

I feel bad for thinking that at this moment in time. But I'm a horny teenager who's been lying about having orgies and not actually having any.

His fingers eventually bury themselves in his pockets. He meets my eyes. I can feel the sparks, the explosiveness of him traveling between us. We breathe and we breathe and we breathe. And I realize that I don't want to be a bitch to Tristan anymore.

I want to— Oh, god. I don't even know what I want to do.

"Shit" is all he says.

"Yeah," I reply. "I'm coming down now." I fix him with a look of pure poison. "Don't let me fall."

He knows what I mean. If I fall, it will be like a Pick Me Up.

I throw myself onto the window, throw my legs over the edge. He takes a few steps back, and I can't help but roll my eyes a little. I know I'm moving with a bit more verve than usual, but did I really look that bad before?

"What?" I glare at him.

"Nothing, nothing." He shakes his head. "Just, you're back to being a bitch. So I know everything's normal."

He grins, and I try to grin back. But it feels like I'm splintering into a million little pieces. I can't stop thinking about Amy. About the fact that it may not have been a suicide.

"Right," I say, trying not to dwell on it.

I twist my body around to start sliding down when I catch sight of something. "Shit!" I reach out and grab the inside edge of Mark's window. Splinters, cutting into the palm of my hand. About ten of them.

"Hang on, there's something I have to see," I call to Tristan.

"Well, I'm enjoying what I'm seeing," he says. I can practically hear the laughter in his voice, and realize that he probably has a very unflattering view of my ass right now.

"Fuck you," I growl as I haul myself up, back through the window as ungracefully as the last time. I'm obviously not made for petty crime such as breaking and entering.

I stumble into the room and across the carpet like a drunk in heels. There's something hanging on the back of Mark's door. He's taped a message to it.

PETAL. ELLA.

It's addressed to us, in capital letters. The sight of our names, in bright red was what caught my eye before. Another one of Mark's cryptic clues, and I don't know what the hell it means yet.

The words beneath our names: GONE FISHING.

Under that is a picture of a fish chewing on what I can only guess is some bread crumbs.

Mark. Has. Gone. Fishing.

Mark's not exactly the sit-in-a-boat-for-ten-hours type. Because, if nothing bites, he'll be bored as hell and just jump into the water or some shit.

Except. Apparently, he's gone fishing, for an extended period of time. Otherwise he wouldn't have felt the need to inform the world. He's planning to be gone long enough that we'd come here looking for him.

"What the hell?"

I rip the piece of paper from the door, fold it into a tiny square, and slip it into my pocket. Then I slip-slide-fall my way out the window again. Tristan catches me, and he's just sort of holding me. Our faces are so close and I think he's going to kiss me and allmythoughtscrashtogether like ice cubes in a glass of whiskey.

But he doesn't kiss me in the end. He just puts me down and half turns away, looking awkward. Smelling of gunpowder.

His hands are stuck in his pockets again. "So, um, what was it?"

"I'll tell you on the way to Petal's house. We need a car. Do you happen to have one?"

He shakes his head a few times and then says quickly, "Ella. Breaking and entering, okay. Cool. But grand theft auto, not so much."

I punch him on the shoulder and wink. "I'll make a criminal of you yet."

"I have a car," he says. "I have a car. If we walk to my house."

But he seems so nervous. So fucking nervous.

"You don't have to come— You could just give me the car—"

"I'm fucking coming. Deal with it," he snaps.

Chapter Twenty-nine

*T*EN MINUTES LATER, WE'RE STANDING IN FRONT OF TRISTAN'S house. It's not what I imagined. Somehow—I suppose it was the constant smell of gunpowder—I was expecting something grittier. I thought my Explosive Boy would live in a bomb of a house.

But his house is a suburban dream. Red bricks, ivy. Fucking lattices, and lace in the windows. Only the picket fence isn't white; it's blue. I glance at it and raise my eyebrows. "Subversive, dude," I say.

"Dude?" he returns. "Since when do you speak like a pothead?"

"Since now, obviously."

"Come on, the car's in the garage."

We head over, and Tristan pops open the garage door, revealing his wheels.

I lean back a little and whistle. Well, his house may not be a bomb, but his car sure is.

He shakes his head at me. "Unimpressed, I see, Princess Ella."

"Understatement. I'm like anti-impressed. Kids who smell like gunpowder should drive good cars, in my opinion."

"Gunpowder? What is up with you and all this gunpowder shit?"

"Come on," I say. "You mean you haven't noticed that you smell like you wear fucking matchsticks for cologne?"

"No." He bites his lip. Bites it and bites it and bites it and doesn't say anything. "No," he repeats finally. Heavily.

"Let's go to Pet's, okay?" I say to break the silence.

He nods and walks me around to the side of the car. Opens the door. "Come on, Princess."

He's mocking me. So I mock him right back. Fluttering eyelashes. Stepping as if I'm walking on balloons. "Coming, Prince Charming."

I slide into the seat. He's laughing as he walks to the other side of the car. He gets into the driver's seat, and his hand shifts to the gear stick. Before he can move it, I close my own fingers around it. Meet his eyes.

"Call me princess one more time, and I *will* knee you in the balls."

He just laughs. Guns the engine. It roars and guzzles and sputters to life like a monster. And then we're pulling out of the driveway. The car cruises, not smoothly, but it's still cruising. There's still sunshine on black roads. There's still that sticky, mellow feeling you get from being in a car on a fairly warm day.

I lean back, forget for a second, and Tristan lets me. He doesn't break the quiet with words; but his fingers drum, drum, drum against the wheel as he drives.

But every good thing has to end. Eventually, he has to ask a question. "Instructions, please? I haven't been stalking Petal, so I dunno how to get to her house."

I laugh. "Who have you been stalking?" I ask. "Didn't take you for a stalker."

He sighs. "Well, damn that," he drawls. "It was always my aim to be taken for a stalker. Seriously, though. Directions, please."

I open my eyes with a sigh. Look around. We're on the main road in Sherwood. Tristan spins us into the round-about.

"That way," I point. "Then just take every left, and you wind up in front of Petal's house. It's at the end of the cul-de-sac. The ugly yellow house."

"Complimentary."

"Oh," I laugh. "It's beautiful on the inside. Petal's family just doesn't give a fuck about appearances."

Unlike mine. Unlike my perfect mother, who had to do all that PR damage control after Amy died since Dad was nowhere to be seen. But instead of calling with condolences, the assholes she works with had lectures on their lips. Alcohol? Why did your daughter have alcohol?

My mother should have been honest. She should have said, "I was in fucking DC and my husband was god knows where and we don't really know."

Instead, she'd rattle off her spiel about "youthful indiscretions." She had it memorized, and, word for word for word, she gave it to everyone who called. As if I were some business document. As if I'd become work.

I didn't even have Amy to rant to about it.

"You okay?"

We've made it to Petal's house without me even noticing the roads flying by. "Yeah. Fine."

My placebo pill—word.

I am *finefinefinefine* all the way to the door. When we get there, I can't move. We stand there and stand there. Eventually, Tristan gives two sharp raps against the peeling wood with his knuckles.

The door swings open ten seconds later. It's Petal's brother. He's twentysomething, and we made out once during a game of spin the bottle at a party. As a result, he can barely stand to look at me. He flushes red. "Um, hi," he says.

"Hey." I stare, hold his gaze, and watch him squirm.

I feel so stupid, but I can't help myself. I just do it and

do it until he coughs and then I look away, and my eyes are burning as if I'm about to cry again. I turn them down, toward the planks of the porch, as he says, "I'll get Petal for you."

I nod and keep on staring at the planks. His footsteps make soft thuds against the wood floors as he walks off.

I let myself breathe deeply.

"You okay?"

I wish Tristan wasn't so concerned. It reminds me of everything I am, of everything I'm not.

Of the little girl I once was, the little girl I've lost.

I sniff, and my gaze bores farther down into the scratchy wood of the porch. And I can feel Tristan's hand on my shoulder, and I can tell that he knows I'm not okay. My head, it wants to collapse onto his shoulder and just rest there.

But I have to pull it the fuck together. I have to pull it together, because I can hear footsteps again, and they're lighter and quieter this time. Petal. I need to keep this up, keep the nuts and bolts plugged into my IKEA kitchen personality for a little bit longer.

Just until she breaks, or Mark breaks.

Just until I know whether one of them pushed Amy.

I raise my head, stare at the space framed by the door's dark wood edges. Fix my gaze on the white wall with cracks spidering across it.

In my peripheral vision, I see Petal emerging in the doorway.

Petal's here. She's here, and I can play coy bitch with her even though I don't really want to.

Mark's camera has a gray strap; I slip my finger through it and twirl it in the air. Once, twice, three times. Petal catches sight of the camera, and her eyes widen. She says my name as if it's an explanation for everything. "Ella—"

She covers her mouth, and it sounds like she's choking, and then she's spitting out "Amy, Amy, Amy" as if she's drowning and she needs to cough up water before she can suck in air.

And then she's out the door, and the door is closed. Quiet as a whisper, she slides down the wood, through the peeling paint, onto the wooden deck. Dust flies up from around her butt.

"What happened, Petal?" I want to drag her to her feet. I want to seize her by the collar and scream, "Did you fucking push Amy? Did you fucking push Amy?" But she looks so pathetic that I can't. My body won't.

My heart won't let me.

We stand there, and the silence roars with Petal's sobs. Her hand hovers over her stomach as if it's hollow.

I want to hug her. But I won't, won't, won't.

I have to keep this up; I have to do this. Just a little

longer, just a few more pushes. I just need the truth and then I can stop.

My voice wavers as I say, "Why did she jump?" And now it's me who's begging. I'm begging her to tell me what I want to hear. That there was a rational explanation for the most irrational of actions.

And the pain is so great. The pain is worse than the splinters that still dig into my skin. It's so bad that snippets of memory start to fly back to me.

I won't let go. I won't let go. I won't let go. Her hand is in mine. And then she stands and drags me up with her.

Everything goes blurry. Faded lights. Shouting. Voices, voices, voices. Words punching through the dark.

Then. Then her body sails through the air. The wind rushes up from beneath her. Jacket soaring up like a fucking parachute. For a second I think it will save her, that she'll float. But only for a second.

Thwack. *I close my eyes. Open them.*

She sprawls in the grass. In front of the fucking gnome.

"She jumped because she was fucked up," Petal says, disrupting my memory. "She jumped because she wanted to die."

I don't believe it. I can't believe it. There's this tug-of-war within me. It's like every cell in my body has been split in two, and each half is screaming different things at the other. The first half yells that Petal's telling the truth, that she wouldn't lie. And the second half is yelling, screaming, crying that I had Amy's hand.

Her fingers were knotted through mine.

I would not have let her go.

"I didn't let her go." I run my fingers through my hair. "Pet, she didn't jump. She couldn't have jumped. Something must've happened, because I didn't let go of her."

"No," Petal whispers. "No, you didn't. Shit, Ella. I can't tell you this. Go ask Mark. We decided—if you ever asked, ever remembered—he'd be the one to say."

"You planned this?" My anger blazes like a bonfire.

But then her voice is so soft that it turns my heart into a big puddle of water. "We wanted to protect you, Ella. Trust me, if I could forget, I would. If I could choose not to remember, I would."

"You don't get it." I pace up and down her porch now, on the verge of tearing my hair out. I make do with snapping every single stray thread on the bottom of my T-shirt. They're unraveling, anyway; I'm just helping things along. "You don't get what it's like not knowing. It's so fucking— it's like . . . I don't even know, Petal. It's crap, utter shit. Please tell me."

But she just looks at me—looks *through* me. She's seen a ghost.

"Where's Mark?" she says eventually.

"Mark's gone fishing."

Petal stares at me.

She looks so helpless. A leaf tossed around in summer winds. Petal, who throws punches with her handbag when other girls get in her way in the lunch line. Petal, who gave James Talen a black eye because he *dared* to call Amy fat.

The backs of my eyes sting with tears. How the fuck can I think it was her fault? Mark's? The people who were always there for Amy.

Because all the signs in my memory are pointing at them, that's why.

And suddenly, Petal's springing to her feet. "We have to find him," she announces.

"Well, no shit, Sherlock," I drawl. Because even now I want to keep my cool. I need to keep my shit together.

I am *fine*.

"No," she says. She runs toward Tristan's car. Like actually, literally, sprints to it and rattles the door handle, trying to get it open. "No, you don't get it. *Gone fishing*." She says it as if I'm the slow one. "Mark's gone to the lake. Mark's gone to the lake, Ella—"

The lake. Fuck.

I run to the car and Tristan follows me, unlocking the doors. We all pile into the car.

"God, Tristan, I don't know if you have enough gas, but I need you to take us to Lake Longshore."

"Why?" he says, but he's already driving. "Try not to zone out this time, Ella. I need directions."

I open my mouth, but Petal beats me to an explanation. "He loved it. He loved it way too much; that was the problem. It was his zen place, his perfect place; and ever since he's been vanishing there. And he started to go for longer and longer and—"

He never told me about his photography. He never really tells us about his feelings. He never speaks about what's going on in his head. I have no idea why he's doing this. Why is he running away?

Because that's what he's doing. That's what "gone fishing" means.

But then I realize that this is, in a way, a second chance for me. I couldn't save Amy, didn't notice her when she was crying out to be noticed, because it hurt me too much. I didn't want to understand her. But now, even though I'm spitting mad at Mark, I want to know what's going on in his head.

Silence stretches in the car like a coastline, as far as the eye can see.

"And?" Tristan says, eventually breaking it. His knuckles are white against the steering wheel.

"About a week before he made one of his many resolutions to get clean, Mark went out to the lake," I say, picking up where Petal left off. This is me being brave; this is me communicating instead of simply talking. "He just sat there. He was gone for almost two days and then Amy got this text: 'Gone fishing. Lake Longshore.' It was like he suddenly remembered that people might be worried about him."

I shake my head. There was this glazed look on Mark's face when we got there. He was so out of it, dirt streaked across his face. Dirt under his fingernails and his eyes so wide. He didn't want to come back home.

He said something was going on with his family, but he wouldn't tell us what.

Petal offered to let him stay with her, but he shook his head no. He said, "I couldn't impose on you like that," as if he were forty and she was some stranger instead of his best friend.

I didn't even know he had language like that in him.

About ten seconds later, he broke down. Because it's easy enough to pretend that you're growing up when you're ten and so much harder to actually do it at seventeen.

Back then it was Amy who held him, Amy who kissed his tears away—what fucking bullshit that seems like now—and then he said, "If I ever want to run away, you'll know where to find me. I'll ditch my stuff here and then head out, because I'm a dickhead like that."

Joking tone. Serious eyes.

We chose to trust the tone over the eyes.

Tristan remains silent, but I notice his knuckles whiten even more. I notice that the engine roars a little louder, notice our pace picking up.

We need to reach Mark before he ditches his stuff and runs.

I don't know how long it's been since he left, but hopefully we can get to him before he's halfway to another state.

I can't let him run away. I don't want to lose another friend.

I turn my head so that it's facing out the window and no one will see my tears but the blue sky, the parched grass, and the road signs.

Chapter Thirty

*W*E RUN OUT OF GAS WITH A GAS STATION IN SIGHT, DAN-gled in front of us like a carrot.

"What now?" Petal says, climbing out of the car and slamming the faded, scratched blue door shut.

"We push," I say.

Because that's all there is for us. We just have to keep on pushing.

Tristan rolls his eyes. "No," he says. "Someone—me, probably—runs up there and gets a bit of gas in one of those can things and comes back with it."

"Why *you*?" Petal's eyes have narrowed. She slaps her hand against the side of the car, and the metal sound clangs over the road, through the sky. "Because you think if I sit here with Ella I'll snap and tell her everything?" Her face turns red. Her beautiful, porcelain features scream their rage and fear at us.

She shakes her head. "No way. I'm getting the gas. I'm getting the fucking gas."

I open my mouth, but before I can speak she's walking away. I turn to Tristan. He's staring after her. Watching the way her hair swishes, and the back of her jeans. Petal has the most beautiful everything I've ever seen—and that includes the most beautiful huffy walk.

Tristan is totally perving on her, and for some odd reason that makes me incredibly jealous. Shit. No, I can't *like* Explosive Boy.

I don't. No way.

Okay, well, maybe there's a way.

But I don't *want* to like him, because he thinks he can save me. And I don't want to be saved. I want to be left to fall.

Tristan's such a stupid, stubborn idiot. But I like him, I do; and somehow this makes me clench my fists. This makes me get ready to side-kick like they taught me in Tae Kwon Do classes in the eighth grade.

Because people, they hurt you. When you like them, when you admit to liking them, it's like saying *game over*. It's like giving them a gun and saying, *You now have the option of putting a bullet through my heart, okay? Cool.*

I don't want to give Tristan that gun. Not now, not ever.

I can't stand having Tristan so close to me anymore.

Can't stand the warmth that I can feel between his jeans and mine. The almost-there touch of his loosely curled fingers.

I lean back against the car, sliding to the ground and kicking my legs out across the road.

"Ella, I know this isn't a highway or anything, but I'm pretty sure people still use it."

"And?"

"Do you want your limbs to get ripped off by a truck?"

"Maybe."

He runs his fingers through his explosive hair. "Right. It's you. I shouldn't have asked that."

Tristan refrains from giving me a lecture, although I'm pretty sure it's killing him on the inside. He takes a few shaky steps and then collapses beside me.

He wriggles his right foot, and a sock-covered toe pops out of a hole in his faded brown sneaker.

"Gross." But I laugh.

"If a car comes, race you back to the grass?"

There are fields, big wide expanses of grass edging the side of the road. The green just seems to roll on forever until it hits a few ant-sized houses in the distance. "Okay," I say, trying to fight the feeling that this game is almost as bad as Pick Me Ups.

A car comes along ten minutes later. A big, black, thrumming machine made of speed and muscle and power. Well, okay, maybe I'm exaggerating a little. Maybe it's just as much of a bomb as Tristan's car.

But that doesn't stop the adrenaline inside me from pumping, pushing, pulsing through my body. Falling into the cracks that spiderweb along the surface of the road, infusing the whole world with a roar of feeling that spurs me to get to my feet.

And then we're sprinting. Tristan and I, getting off the road at the last possible moment. A blur of black whips by, and there's the sound of a horn going off. Again and again and again and again. Shit, I think we freaked out the driver.

I slide my hand over my eyes and squint after the car, trying to make sure that its driver hasn't spun off the road or something. More guilt is not what I need right now.

Fingernails, digging into palms. I feel the splinters that are still spiked through my skin from when I nearly broke Mark's window frame.

I don't feel guilt. I don't feel sadness. I cannot fucking feel the tears crawling down my face.

I flop onto the grass, wipe the tears away with the flats of my hands before Tristan can see them. Before he lowers himself down beside me far more gracefully.

"How long do you think Petal's going to be?" I ask.

"A while. Carrying a gallon of gas two miles is probably going to be hard for her."

We're quiet for a moment; and for the first time since I've known Tristan, the silence isn't punctuated by coughs, shuffling, or fingers twisting in and out of each other. Instead, there's the chirping of birds and the distant sounds of the highway.

The sun slants across my face, blisters my shoulders, and I am still. I am still, and I try to make my stomach stop writhing and be still with me. But it won't go away. I'm becoming aware for about the hundred millionth time that Tristan doesn't have to be here with me. He doesn't have to be here at all.

I roped him into this, and I can't help but break the peaceful silence to ask, "Tristan, why are you so hell-bent on helping me?"

And this is me asking the important questions. The ones I've always wanted to ask in the past but never had the guts to. Instead of asking "Why aren't you eating?" I spent my time asking about the weather.

I'm not making the mistakes I made with Amy again.

I wait for Tristan to reply; and, god, I hope he doesn't tell me that it's because he just wants to get into my pants. Because I don't buy that crappy excuse for being nice. Not for one second, not one little bit.

"Tristan?"

I'm tired of waiting for an answer. He can look gray all he likes, but he will speak.

A sigh whooshes from his lips. More silence. I begin a countdown. Sixty seconds from now I'll say his name again; and if he doesn't respond to that, I'll repeat it in another thirty seconds and so on until he answers me.

For now I wait.

Talk, goddamnit. Why won't he speak?

Sixty seconds. "Tristan." My voice is sharp this time.

He seems to realize I won't let this go, because he closes his eyes and says "You're not going to like it" in a voice that bleeds like a raw wound.

"Hit me with your best shot."

"You're such a cliché," he says, snorting.

"Whatever. Just speak before I kill you."

He laughs. "Okay," he says. "Okay." Resolve. Hard as steel. He is no longer coming undone. "I want to—*help* you, first off because I'm incredibly selfish. I'm the new kid, and you were the most interesting person at Sherwood High. But also because I have this problem. I like to—save people."

"Um. What?"

I'm so confused right now. I'm interesting? He likes to save people? He says it as if it's a freaking hobby. I imagine him writing it down on his college apps: *On rainy afternoons what do you enjoy? I, Tristan Explosive Boy, enjoy* saving *people.*

It takes everything I have not to laugh.

A lady beetle settles on my knuckles, its light, ticklish movement unfurling my fist. As soon as I move, the beetle zooms off into the sunny day. I wish I could be as carefree as that beetle.

"Okay," Tristan says, sitting up, burying his face in his hands, speaking from between his fingers. "It's like this. You remember how I told you about my brother? About how he died?"

I nod. "Yeah."

"Of an overdose. I was such a fucking coward. I could have saved him; I could have stopped him. But when he came to me, crying, and told me that his life was going down the toilet because of the cancer and the way his limbs wouldn't obey him anymore and the crappiness of the chemo—when he told me all of that, I didn't say, 'Hey Ethan, let's go and make your life fun. I'll fight this with you.'

"I took the easy way out. I let him convince me—and god, it took a lot of convincing—to get him the pills."

I can feel my eyes widening.

Tristan is crying now. He's sobbing, and his face is still buried in his hands. Tears stream around his fingers. His voice sounds like he's being strangled. "I didn't . . . I didn't just let my brother go when I could have hung on to him. I gave him the gun to shoot himself with. And, yeah, I've spent the past two years in juvie paying for it. But it's not enough; a lifetime's worth of penance wouldn't be enough."

He shakes his head, and tufts of his explosive hair flutter into the sky. His ember hair seems too tired to even really burn. His shoulder blades spike up through his shirt and then fall and then spike up again. Earthquakes, sobs wrack his body.

For a second I'm frozen with horror at what he's been through, what he's done. It floods through my body like glue, sticking my lips together, stitching my muscles up. I gasp for breath. He reaches out a hand to stroke the side of my cheek but then drops it.

"So now you know why I like to save people. It's because when it counted most, I couldn't save the one person I loved more than anyone else in this entire world." His eyes are still closed, but he opens them as he speaks his next words. "I loved my brother. They didn't mention that in the headlines when they called me a murderer. When they said the judge was a bastard for giving me two years *only.*

"You can't even look at me, can you, Ella?"

And then I force myself to unfreeze, let the sunlight thaw me and wash all the glue from my system. "I can look at you." I twist my head, sharply, and meet his eyes. This time he's the one who turns away. "Look at me. Fuck you, look at me."

Swearing always does the trick.

And there's no time to think it over, so I do what I know in my bone marrow he was going to do ten seconds ago. I lean forward, brush my fingers against his cheek. We're close, so close.

I can see the red that rims his eyes, the pink of his lips. *Kiss me,* they seem to shout. So I do.

And at first he tastes bitter. But then he opens his mouth a little, and I can taste the gunpowder mixed with some kind of musky cologne.

The kiss deepens.

He falls backward, topples onto the soft grass. I go down with him, head resting on his chest, sunshine resting on my back. I plant a kiss on his chin. God, I feel like an absolute idiot doing it. But I want to, and ever since Amy died I've been all about seizing moments.

I lift my head, meet Tristan's eyes. "It wasn't your fault," I say. "It was not your goddamn fault. You were fourteen."

He laughs softly, his fingers running through grass. "Fourteen is not that young."

"You were trying to help him," I whisper, surrendering

all my toughness to the summer day.

Amy's question from that night rings in my mind: *Why are you a bitch, Ella?*

Now I know why I couldn't answer that question properly. It's because I'm not. I'm not nice, but I'm not a bitch, either. I'm just fucking average. I'm just like everybody else.

"Tristan—" Sometimes there aren't any words. Sometimes all you can do is say someone's name, let it fall into the air between you.

His eyes close. His arm comes up, slides around my back, and he practically crushes me in a one-armed hug. "Yeah, but it was just so goddamn stupid."

He's warm. Warmer than the sunlight even. It's nice, because I've been cold for so long. I'm hyperaware of the fact that we're touching practically everywhere. My hip rocks into his. Our knees knock together.

I make conversation to distract myself. "I'm jealous of you," I tell him in that hushed-whisper voice people use when they're making confessions.

"Seriously? Why? I'm such a fuckup."

I squeeze the hem of his shirt between my fingers. Twist, twist, twist. "Because you're so . . . yourself, you know?"

"Who else am I supposed to be?" He laughs, puts on a pirate accent as he says, "Captain Jack Sparrow?"

Explosive Boy, I want to tell him. That's who he's supposed to be. Someone who's far more James Dean than he really is. But I guess I'm supposed to be a lot bitchier than I am, too.

"I don't know," I say. "I feel like I don't ever . . . I developed this mask when I was a freshman, and it's like I wore it for so long that I forgot to take it off. And now I don't know what's underneath it."

"I can't believe you just said that," he says.

"Why?"

"Because it's *you*. Expressing emotional insecurity. Quick—duck and take cover; the apocalypse is about to begin!"

"Very funny," I say, tracing circles on the back of his shirt. Biting my lip.

He catches my hand. "Stop freaking out about it, Ella."

"About what?"

"Who you are."

"But don't you think that we have to figure it out so that we can be, I don't know, happy?"

I blush. Admitting that I want, need to be happy feels somehow shameful. He's right. I'm shit, shit, shit at reaching out to people.

He shakes his head. "You can't define yourself as any one thing. You'll change over time, you know?" He smiles.

"'Do I contradict myself? Very well, then I contradict myself. I am large, I contain multitudes.' It's Whitman," he says. "I'm not that smart."

So on top of everything else, he quotes Whitman in conversation. "I didn't take you for an English nerd." But then I didn't take him for anything else, either. I didn't acknowledge that he could contain multitudes—that he could be leather jackets and red hair and gunpowder cologne and twenty-first-century chivalry and a Kid Whisperer and a selfish saver of people.

What contradictions will emerge in me once I let go of my need to define everything about myself? Once I learn to just *be*.

"Give me another quote," I say.

But before he can reply, something clatters to the ground behind us. A throat is cleared and then cleared again, and then there's a loud cough. A foot tap, tap, tapping against the asphalt.

I know it's Petal, but I don't want to move because this moment is so peaceful. It's like a piece of quiet I can fold away into my soul.

Petal can't take the sight of us—limbs tangled through each other's, lying in the grass—any longer. "So, um, clearly, I'm interrupting something!"

I get up quickly, in one fluid movement. "Oh, Pet. You should have said you were here," I say sweetly.

She takes one look at the expression on my face. "Well, while you two are hooking up, Mark is—" She doesn't want to say what Mark's doing. Because she doesn't know, and she'd rather not speculate. Me, too.

"Get up," I tell Tristan. "There's still someone you can save."

Petal and I get in the car, while Tristan tries to pour the gas into the tank. It looks hard, without one of those funnel thingies.

His eyes are redder than hell in the rearview mirror, and Petal's pretending not to notice. But she keeps glancing at him every ten seconds, so it's not like she's convincing anyone. The thing that surprises me is what I see in her eyes when they take him in.

Concern.

I'd forgotten that she was—is—the most caring person I know. Despite the bitchiness, when anyone truly needs her, Petal's there.

And suddenly, I need to know that he's okay, too. "I'll be right back," I tell Petal.

The ground is still warm, and the grass waves in a gentle breeze. Gas sloshes and slips over Tristan's fingers as he tips the container into the gas tank. Some of it drip, drip, drips onto the black surface of the road. The sun turns it into a shimmering rainbow patch.

It's odd how appearances can change so quickly. Just minutes ago I thought Tristan was trying to save me, rescue me. But now I know that he's really trying to save himself.

I tear up as I watch him crying. Pouring gas into the tank.

"You okay?"

"Fine," he says, throwing my own placebo at me.

I nod, even though I know he's lying. "Okay." I turn to head to the car when the smell of gunpowder catches me. I can't help myself. "Why do you smell of gunpowder?" I ask. "And what the fuck were you doing on the football field that day before I met you?"

I'm aware that I sound like a stalker asking that last question. But I need to ask it. Otherwise the image of him windmilling his arms through mud will haunt me forever.

He chuckles, but it sounds fake.

"It's not really a funny reason," he says. "I smell of gunpowder because when we were younger, Ethan and I used to go camping all the time. We spent most of our time lighting matches and trying to start campfires. Plus, Ethan loved to burn incense.

"We used to burn a few sticks every night and just talk. I still do both. The campfires, whenever I can. The incense, every night. I guess that's why I smell like gunpowder."

"And the football field?"

He turns red. "I can't believe you saw that," he mutters. "I was being a dumbass. You know how sometimes you get all dumb and metaphorical?"

"Um—" I don't, really. But I can pretend to. "Yeah."

"I wanted the rain to wash me out. And I wanted the mud to be, like, ironic soap. Because it was my first day in the new town, at the new school, you know. I wanted myself to be a blank slate."

"That makes no sense; you know that."

"What can I say? I'm highly illogical," he says with a grin before he returns his attention to the gas. When he's done, the container slips from his fingers to the road.

"Are you disappointed that I'm not some dangerous gangster or some shit?" he asks.

"No, I'm not disappointed." And then I flash my cheesiest smile. "You *contain multitudes*, and nothing says sexy bad boy like *multitudes*."

My comment shakes a laugh out of him, but he's still got this hangdog expression on his face.

"Tristan," I say before we get in the car, because I feel a stupid-insane need to repeat this, "it wasn't your fault."

"It was. Sometimes the people around us go, and it's our fault. And we just have to accept it and move on. I'll move on eventually."

He smiles, such a peaceful smile. But it's like a gunshot through my stomach, and I'm the one bleeding now.

I clutch my stomach. He gets into the car, but I stand there and stand there and stand there. Finally, he rolls down the window and says with a sigh, "Get in."

And then I move as if I'm made of water. I slosh around in the front seat as he drives us to Lake Longshore.

Sometimes the people around us go, and it's our fault.

Chapter Thirty-one

THE IDEA THAT I PUSHED AMY, OR EVEN JUST LET HER GO, eats away at my stomach throughout the trip.

Strip of blue sky. *I pushed her.*

Smell of cow shit. *I let go of her.*

Tree branches spiraling away into twigs and then leaves. *I pushed her.*

Stop sign. No way, go back sign. *I let go of her.*

And the sign's right. There is no way to go back.

I just need that last little snippet of memory to tell me what I already know.

I want to ask Petal, get her to trigger the memory for me. But if, as I suspect, I'm the one who pushed Amy, then she and Mark have been protecting me all this time. So I kind of owe her for that.

The roads beneath us have grown bumpy. Been nearly two hours since we left now.

They had Amy's funeral somewhere out here—the

one her family wouldn't let us come to. Maybe this is Mark's sick way of saying good-bye to the only girl he ever loved.

Amy's words float back to me. *I've never really* loved *Mark. He was always just the next best. . . . I wanted* you.

But Mark would never push Amy off a building no matter how angry he was. Would he? Would I?

All I know when I think of Mark's shallow dimples and his stupid scarves and the way he used to enjoy doing flips on the trampoline in my yard is that I can't let him go, too. I will never, ever let him or Petal go.

So we drive down the bumpy roads chasing after Mark. And we've got five miles to go, and then it's four miles.

Three. Two. One.

The lake looms. Most lakes are vast and endless. Not this one. It's nothing more than a play pool—okay, maybe three or four play pools—embedded between craggy rocks and leafy trees. Rocks skid beneath my feet as I get out of the car.

Run. Run. Run.

I lengthen my stride.

Hope to god that Mark's still here. We have to find him.

Tristan and Petal keep pace, and we round yet another bend together.

And there he is, sitting on a rock. Completely hunched over, body swaying toward the glassy surface of the water.

"Mark!" I call.

Bad move. He whips around and sees me. His eyes are redder than Tristan's were beside the road.

Shit, he really wants to run away from all this.

I hop-skip-jump over and between the rocks until I'm beside him. "Marcus Antony Hayden, how *dare* you try and run away?"

God. I've turned into such a cry baby lately. The tears taste salty as I reach out and grab Mark's hand. My fingers find the spaces between his, and I lace them together, stitch us together. This time I will not let go.

He just laughs at me, though. "What makes you think it's going to work this time, Ella? You held on to Amy; but it didn't help her, did it?"

His words wind me. I sink onto the rock and let the world, the lake float in little pieces around me. Everything disappears. Everything is engulfed by the hazy, dizzy feeling that takes over. Everything. I held her hand, and it didn't help her? Because I let go? Because I pushed her?

Because I'm a murderer?

Mark didn't say it like that. He said it like "You tried your best and you failed."

"Tell me what happened, goddamn you." I don't remove my right hand from his, but I hit him with my left. It's an awkward blow that glances off his chest. "I just want to know."

I fight the tears from my voice. I am strong. I've got it together.

I'm not falling apart.

Deep breath. Deep breath.

"You want to know. Fuck, Ella. Don't make me tell you this. It's not—*pretty.*"

"I killed her, didn't I? I killed her. Oh, my god." Trembling fingers against my lips and sobs and sobs and sobs.

Tristan drops his hand onto my shoulder from behind. "What do you mean? Ella, don't say that."

I turn to Petal for support, but she's leaning forward, over the lake. She decorates it with vomit.

When she comes back up, she says, "You didn't kill Amy, Ella." She turns to Mark, eyebrows pulling down, tears dripping from her nose. "Don't make me do this, Mark. You promised. I wanted to tell her immediately when I stopped hiding, because it would hurt too much. And you said . . . you said, if this happened, you'd tell her. You were the one who decided to hide this."

Mark's sneakers scuff against the rock. It's one of the gestures he's had since he was a child. He used to do it when confessing to letting his dog poo in his scary neighbor's yard. He used to pull that face when he'd hacked my e-mail or when he'd alienated some guy I liked. He used to pull that face whenever he wanted a favor, or forgiveness.

I'm not sure which he wants this time. Both, maybe.

His voice is soft, so sad that it scrubs at my skin, wearing me down to the bone. I'm bone weary. We all are. "The reason I didn't want to tell you about how Amy died," he says, biting his lip so hard that I'm scared he's going to bleed, "is because I wanted to save you pain. The reason you can't remember any of it is because, well, we think you got a concussion, Ella—you passed out and all—not that you were drunk out of your mind."

"Then why didn't you take me to the doctor?"

"We . . . didn't want to have to tell you what happened. I wanted to spare you." He manages to sound noble and heroic instead of like the patronizing little nitwit that he is.

It's all snapping into place now. Why Petal came over to my house again so soon after Amy's death. Barely hours later she was checking on me. Seeing whether the concussion was getting the better of me.

She stayed over at my house, and we watched movies together and cried together and fell asleep on the couch. I wonder now, how much of that time she spent actually watching the movies versus just watching me.

The first half of the next day, Petal was with me. And then when she went off to her room to become a phantom, Mark took over.

A week later, he invented Pick Me Ups.

When my body was safe, we found a way to make both of our minds safe.

You can't think when you fall.

Problem is, you can't fall forever. You'll always hit the ground eventually.

I let the information sink in. Absorb it. And hell, it does make some sense—I'm fairly sober in all the memories I've managed to get back so far. Amy is drunk. Mark and Petal and I are more aware of ourselves from what I've managed to piece together.

"Amy pushed me back onto the roof?"

I remember now.

Crack. *My head hits a tile. Another one clatters down; and its sharp, triangular edge hits my forehead.*

Everything goes black.

And then, cutting through the blackness is the wail of a siren. The red alarm flashes, and Mark's whispering "Shhh, shhh" in my ear; but he's sobbing, and I know something is wrong.

I can see stars twinkling above my head. I can feel the grass prickling my back. I don't know where I am, but I force myself upright. Blood rushes to my head. Dizzy, dizzy, dizzy. I push a hand up against the side of my head and gasp.

Mark and Petal are next to me, quietly listening to the sirens. An ambulance pulls up in front of what I recognize as my front garden. For who? Surely not for me? I've done something to my head, but it's not that bad.

I stand so that I'm shoulder to shoulder with Petal, and I'm going to ask her about it; but she turns away from me ever so slightly. Then Mark steps to the side a little, and I see Amy. Twisted. Limbs knotted through my grass, laced through the weeds in front of my gnome. But her hands were laced through mine what seems like seconds ago.

The scream that tears from my throat will never be enough.

It will never be enough.

On the rock, I swallow, gulping down the fear that floats to me from my memories. It's as tangible as the wreaths of smoke above my head at the party, as tangible as the glasses of punch that slid down my throat earlier that night.

"What happened? How did she get there? How did I get there?"

Mark peers at me from beneath lidded eyes. Checks whether I'm okay before nodding and continuing the story. His words shoot straight for once. "There's not much to it, Ella." His sigh shakes the lake, shakes the stars out of the sky. I hadn't noticed it was this late. "You wouldn't let go, so Amy decided that you were collateral damage."

"Huh?" My voice is a sharp knife, but it's twisting into no one's heart but my own.

He closes his eyes. "You wouldn't let go, so she decided it would be okay to drag you down with her. She jumped off the rooftop with your hand still in hers, and didn't give a shit if you came tumbling after. Because she wanted what she wanted, and you were collateral damage."

I gag, but nothing comes up. I slam my palm into my windpipe and wheeze out a "Fuck."

Tristan sits next to me, slips his arms around my waist.

I distract myself for as long as possible by looking at my friends, the sky, the lake. I even examine just how gray the rock is. In the end I have to face up to the cold, hard truth: I didn't kill my best friend; she tried to kill me.

I almost wish it were the other way around. I don't want to hate Amy now that she's in the grave. I miss her like crazy, and I don't want to know this.

"It's not true," I wheeze. I've fucked up my throat. I'm not particularly worried about it, though, to be honest. Pain is my painkiller. "It can't be, or I'd be dead."

"You would be. But I nearly broke your fucking wrist pulling you back. She made her choice, but she shouldn't have dragged—"

What Mark's saying gets lost as the last piece of the jigsaw puzzle slips into place and the last memory surfaces.

She stands up, drags me to my feet with her. "Amy, Ames, what are you doing?"

She just laughs and spins like a ballerina, and I'm forced to jog around her in a circle to avoid falling down. I'm not letting go of her.

"You want to do this with me, don't you, Ella?" She's looking

off the roof again, slurring her words. She leans forward to plant a kiss on my cheek. "You do love me, don't you? You want to come with me."

I feel sick. Sick to my stomach, sick to my soul. I want to throw up over the edge of this roof, not jump.

"No, you want to come with me. Back inside," I say. "I'll get you some water."

Mark's standing behind Amy. He moves forward, ready to grab her. But she's too fast for him, too fast for me.

"You're just frightened, Ella. You'll thank me in the afterlife."

With that she jumps. No, she doesn't just jump. In typical, melodramatic Amy style, she scissors kicks her way off the roof. Terror beats through me as I feel her weight dragging me with her as she goes down.

I try to untangle my fingers from hers, but her grip is so fucking firm. I don't want to die. I don't, I don't, I don't, no matter how much I've thought I wanted to in certain moments. This is not what I want.

But I'm going down, and there's nothing I can do to stop it. The tiles flake away like they're feathers beneath my feet, and there's no way to dig in on a roof.

And then something closes around my wrist. Fingers, anchoring me to the rooftop. "Petal! Petal!" Mark's shouting.

Pet's out of it, not particularly lucid; but something in her finally wakes up. She runs, tiles falling from the roof, and grabs Mark's hand with one arm and wraps the other around the chimney.

Amy's hanging off the roof, suspended in the air.

"Let go of her, Amy," Mark calls. "Let go of her."

And Amy's voice floats back to us. "I can't," she says. "I'm so afraid—I can't do this on my own. I need Ella."

"I fucking need Ella," Mark retorts. "Let go, Amy. Maybe Pet and I can save you, too, you shithead. Remember to try and land on all fours."

She doesn't say anything for a second. Then, "I don't want to be saved!"

Her fingers slip from mine, and I'm aware that I'm whispering, "No, no, no." My tears are practically hosing the roof. And then she's falling, and the strength with which Mark's pulling on my arm tosses me across the roof.

I slide onto the tiles as I watch Amy fall. The world goes black.

I get up as the memory fades away. I don't know what I'm doing, but I leave the others and head back to the car. It takes god knows how long for me to slip over and around the rocks. I make sure to turn back and wave before I disappear from their sight. Just so they know everything's okay. That I'm fine, fine, fine.

Like a fourteen-year-old who's gotten drunk for the first time, I stumble to the car. I'm crying so badly that I barely manage to make out its door, and it takes me at least three minutes to find the handle. When I do, I pull it open and haul myself into the car.

It smells of gunpowder, of Tristan and the nightly wakes he holds for his brother.

I knock my head into the steering wheel and listen to the horn go off every time my body is wracked by a violent sob. The moon smiles down at me, and I want to flip it off. But I know it would make no difference. Not one little bit.

Amy would still be dead.

She would still have tried to kill me.

God, I don't know if I can forgive her. I know I should, because she wasn't herself and she wasn't thinking rationally. But didn't she hear the note of terror in my voice? Didn't she freaking hear how terrified I was?

And if she did, did she just not care?

She wanted me to follow her into the dark.

I run my fingers through my hair and then beneath my eyes to get rid of the tears.

I guess this is why Pick Me Ups triggered my memories. Because Amy pulled me off the roof, and I was free-falling with her. I was falling, hanging over the edge of the roof. I can remember now: the knot of sick-angry-tired-scared rolling around in my stomach just waiting to be puked out.

That's how you feel right before you're about to die. None of that life-flashing-before-your-eyes shit. Thought flees. You're reduced to three things: skin, bone, feeling.

And that's what Pick Me Ups did, too. Well, that plus the exhilaration.

And shit, maybe I didn't lose my memories because I

was concussed or drunk. Maybe I *chose* to forget them. It feels ridiculously possible. Like all I wanted was to paint over what actually happened so I could be in control. So I could write a new story on that blank space.

A story where Amy made sense.

Where the world made fucking sense.

But there is no story where the world makes sense. Especially not the true story.

Amy repulses me.

Someone knocks on the window. I roll it down, still sobbing, still shivering, but trying to get myself under control. It's Tristan. "Can I come in?" he asks as if his car is some kind of sacred place for me.

I guess it is right now.

"Yeah," I say. And he's kind of a sacred person for me right now.

I want to be saved.

Tristan gets into the car, and he's quiet for a moment, fists stuffed into the pockets of his jeans. Finally, he says, "You have to forgive her."

I keep on crying and don't say anything.

"Ella, listen to me. Sometimes people do stupid things." He laughs a little. "I'm a case in point there. Look, when I tried to help my brother—"

"That was different," I interrupt. "He asked you to do that. I fucking begged her to let go of me."

The sobs stop. It's like speaking is a magic cure for the tears. I feel deathly calm now.

"Regardless. She was drunk out of her mind from what you've told me. She was in a crazy place. And I don't know what else she was; but I do know that she was your best friend, and she probably couldn't think through the consequences of what she was doing."

The words are so rational. They sink into my skin, into my pores. I twist in my seat so that I'm facing Tristan and give him a salty kiss on the lips.

"What was that for?"

I shrug. "I couldn't resist your multitudes."

But really, it's so much more than that.

I squeeze my eyes shut.

My stomach twists with guilt, anger, rage. It's like a mixed drink in there, and the only thing this punch hasn't been spiked with is forgiveness. "Tomorrow you will make so much sense. Tomorrow I'll be able to listen," I say. "But right now I just want to be angry."

I'll forgive her tomorrow. I hope.

Chapter Thirty-two

WE DECIDE TO SPEND THE NIGHT AT THE LAKE AND DRIVE back in the morning. Tristan sleeps in the car, but Mark and Petal and I stay outside. Under the stars. None of us has words for one another; but Petal finger-combs my hair, and occasionally Mark skips stones across the lake, and it feels like a few things, just a few things, are right with the world.

They're not lying to me anymore.

In the morning when we reach Sherwood, all I want to do is head home, fall down on my couch or my bed or the floor. Never get up again. But that's not what I do.

Tristan drops off Mark and Petal first, and somehow it feels right that we're the only ones remaining, even though I've known them for years and him for days. He's driving toward my house; but when he gets to a red traffic light,

I unglue my chapped lips and say, "Take me to the child care center, please."

"But Heather doesn't want you to come back—"

"Fuck what Heather wants. This is important."

He gives me a skeptical look, as if he's not sure I can handle any of it, any of my life right now. But then he turns the car around and heads toward the child care center.

I'm still crying at intervals. I can't help it, can't stop myself. My best friend, she fucking tried to kill me; she was that messed up. I'm trying not to fall apart in the front seat of Tristan's car. Trying not to bash my head into the glove box again and again and again like I did with the steering wheel yesterday at the lake.

My entire body feels cold. Ice has stabbed through my skin, sunk into my bloodstream. It's spread throughout my body. God, I'm freezing, freezing, freezing.

Tristan pulls up outside the center. Kills the engine. "What are you going to do?"

"What I should have done ages ago," I say.

What I should have done for Amy when I realized that something was up with her.

I can do this, I tell myself. *I can do what I'm going to do now, and I can know that it is the right thing. I can hope that, maybe, it will make a difference.*

It's the first time in years that I've bothered to wear a seatbelt. I unbuckle it and open the door.

"Do you want me to come with you?" Tristan asks. He's looking at me, and I love that he's looking at me. That he can still look at me as if he cares when I can see in the side mirror that my hair's a bird's nest and my mouth's become an ugly, ugly line of pain.

"No," I say. "I'll be fine on my own."

And for the first time in my life, I think it might be true.

I find Heather sitting on the bench in the corner of the courtyard. The green paint goes well with her pink-and-peach floral blouse. Some kids are curled up at the end of the slide, waiting for their friend at the top to come down and barrel into them.

"Hey," I say when I'm standing in front of Heather. "What are you going to do about Casey?"

"What are you doing here? I thought I told you to get out. I meant to never come back."

"Yeah, I don't care," I say. I'm too cold to care right now. I dig my fingers into the pockets of my jeans, duck my head, and glance at her. She must have noticed how messed up I look, because she's got this curious look on her face and she isn't yelling at me or attacking me.

It doesn't matter. I'm just here to do what I have to.

"What are you going to do about Casey?" I ask her again.

"What do you mean?"

"Something's wrong with her."

"What's wrong?"

I rub a hand over my forehead. "I don't know. Something. Her mother smokes cigarettes when Casey's around and doesn't give a damn. And Casey likes to say the word *fuck* way too much—"

"Bet you taught her that. . . ."

I ignore her shitty comment. "And she's obsessed with her future, and she thinks she's a green-shaped blob, and she doesn't believe in happy endings. She's a ten-year-old nihilist, Heather, and you have to do something about that."

"She's entitled to view the world the way she wants," Heather says. She watches the kids on the slide as if they're the most fascinating things in the world. And maybe they are. Maybe humans, especially children, really are the most fascinating things in the world, because they're cruel and innocent and beautiful and terrible all at once.

And then they grow up into people like me and Amy, and they're just terrible and cruel. And I have to keep speaking, have to convince Heather, because I don't want Casey to lose the parts of her that are innocent and beautiful.

"Sure," I say. "For sure, she's allowed to have her own views. I'm not asking you to teach her to think she'll get a happy ending. I'm asking you to do something to show her that a world without happy endings is still worth it. That *being* is worth it."

"Are you high?" She's standing up now.

"No. I'm not *high.*"

Why is it that when anyone says anything that matters, people assume drugs are part of the equation? I'm brave enough to say stupid philosophical shit without being drunk or high.

"Look, you have to leave—"

"Have you heard that girl laugh?" She has the laugh of a dead girl. The laugh of a dead girl who tried to kill me. A dead girl whom I'm pretty sure I hate right now. "Have you looked at her eyes? You must have noticed that she cries every day? Seriously, I would go to her school with this, but I don't know where it is; and I would go to her mom with this, but to be honest, she freaks me out." I pause, take a deep breath. "So I'm coming to you, because you're trained to deal with kids, and you can get her help."

Heather stares at me. Readjusts her floral blouse. "Well—"

"Just get her help," I say. And I'm so glad, as I walk away from her, that I imitated my mom's meeting-adjourned voice perfectly.

When I get back into the car, I tell Tristan, "Now take me home."

And he says, "What did you do?"

"Stopped Casey from turning into Amy, hopefully." I crash my head back into the headrest and close my eyes.

"So you still love her then?"

"I don't know. Like I said, I'll forgive her. Just not now."

I *think* I'll forgive her, anyway.

Please, god, let me forgive her. Let me forgive her tomorrow, because I can't live with this storm of sadness and anger brewing inside my body. I don't want to remember Amy this way.

Chapter Thirty-three

*T*OMORROW TURNS INTO THE NEXT DAY, WHICH TURNS INTO next week, which turns into next month.

But I do forgive Amy gradually. Bit by bit. With all my memory snapped into place, it's impossible not to remember everything before that cold night. Impossible not to remember more than the fact that she tried to pull me off a roof.

The day she photocopied her homework for me to copy.

The day she taught me how to pick a lock 'cause I was always forgetting my locker key.

The day she spent two hours braiding my hair so that I'd look "pretty" for some guy I've forgotten.

The day she said, seriously, with a poker face and tears in her eyes, "I'm bulimic."

That was why Mark liked her better when she was fat. That was what he was trying to say: Amy, we love you either way. Amy, you don't have to slowly kill yourself, because we love you.

My response to Amy's news? I put my arms around her and squeezed hard, as if that would prevent her from slowly disappearing. I nodded into her shoulder and said, "I've noticed." Because it's hard not to when your best friend begins to turn into a wraith.

I remember all the times I let Amy down. The time I was supposed to wait for her at the movies when we were twelve, and I got impatient because she was five minutes late. I left without her. I left my friend behind, practically stood her up.

The time I spilled coffee all over her favorite book, and she just laughed it off. And of course, that time in ninth grade when I waged war with Amy over some stupid boy we both liked. She got together with Mark later that month, and it all blew over.

The memories flit into my mind, each one a little piece of sunlight pushing away the overwhelming black hate. Piece by piece by piece it disappears.

Tristan helps, too, by being his softly logical self.

He drives me home now. We're going out or something—I'm not really sure what to call it. It's not as if we can tell people "See, we enjoy saving each other." And Mark puts up with it, even though sometimes I can see from the way he looks at my Explosive Boy that he'd rather punch him in the gut than on the shoulder. That he'd rather say "Fuck you" than "Hey, man."

Mark has a hard time getting over things. Kinda like me.

It happens one morning as I'm about to head to school. I feel at peace with Amy.

Mom's sitting on the couch, dressed in a blue suit, puzzling over a crossword in the newspaper. When she hears my feet creaking over the wooden floors, she looks up and smiles. "You look happy this morning," she says, tilting her head to one side. "It's a good look for you, honey."

Mom has surprised me by not giving up on me after that night when I told her to leave me alone. She has continued to try and worm her way into my life. She still doesn't feel like a mother to me—we're not close, but we manage to exchange words beyond *hello*s and *good-bye*s these days without fighting. She's been kind enough to not make me see Roger, despite my departure from the child care center.

I've told her that only I can put myself back together. She doesn't believe me, but she's giving me a trial period. No truanting, no bruises, no blood. But if I slip up—or rather, fall down—it's off to Roger with me.

"Do you need a lift?"

"No, it's okay. Tristan's picking me up," I say.

She purses her lips, because she doesn't exactly approve

of Tristan. But she doesn't say anything, just takes a sip of her orange juice. She's giving me my space these days, not trying to barge her way in after ignoring me for years.

"Hey, Mom," I say to the back of her head as I walk behind the couches to the foyer. "Thanks, you know, for making an effort with me lately."

She's trying harder than Dad, at the very least. He's taken up a job in a different state. It's been weeks since I've spoken to him, because to be honest, it's too painful to hear the disappointment in his voice. The disappointment that, even from a state away, seems so endless. I don't know if he's disappointed in me or Mom or himself. Maybe all three. I guess I understand in some ways. How do you keep on going when you've watched so many of your dreams die?

Mom turns to face me. "I'm so glad to hear you say that," she says. To someone who didn't know her, her voice would still sound glossy, but I can tell that it's lost a layer of its usual polish. "Have a nice day."

"You, too."

And then I'm out the front door.

I get into Tristan's car, and the smell of gasoline and gunpowder envelopes me. Every time I get into this car, I remember the day I found out what Amy did. I remember banging my head against Tristan's steering wheel, honking the horn, and willing my thoughts to stop, stop, stop.

And every day when I've remembered this, there's this pinch of resentment in my chest. How could Amy do that to me?

Today, all I can think is that our friendship was always flawed. Our friendship was weathered wood at the beach, salt worming its way into the cracks. Everything eroding. It's not like I didn't know that before. And it's not like she wasn't drunk off her ass.

She didn't know what she was doing. She just loved me like anything—and she didn't want to be alone.

I will never forgive her for what she did to herself. But I will forgive her for what she did to me.

"I forgive her."

"Who?" Tristan sounds confused.

"Amy."

"Oh." He eases his foot onto the accelerator and pulls out of my driveway.

Silence. Beneath us, wheels slice across the road. Above us, birds wheel across the sky. At the first traffic light, Tristan asks, "Do you think Ethan forgives me?"

I smile and nod. "He may even be thankful. It was his choice, Tristan, and it seems like he had good reason. He was going, anyway; he just picked his own terms is all."

Tristan nods, but his eyes disappear into the landscape, into the trees in the distance that look like purple bruises against the mist-white sky. Sometimes I sit in on the wakes he holds for Ethan. We just sit in Tristan's room, arms around each other, watching smoke curl away from the incense sticks that his dead brother used to love.

Sometimes Tristan can't hold back his tears, and the words flow out of him because he's overflowing and can't keep them in. Sometimes he'll whisper, "My fault."

Deep down, I think he knows it isn't his fault. But he needs to think it is, because it's easier to blame himself than it is to blame his brother. Because admitting he's not at fault would mean admitting that his brother shouldn't have put him in that position in the first place.

It's hard to admit you're guiltless sometimes, because it also means you're not at all in control. I would know. Sometimes I still try to persuade myself that I killed Amy. I pushed her; she didn't pull me. It was my fault. If only I hadn't—

But there are so many *if only*s, and it never changes reality.

I want to do something for Amy. I want to say goodbye to her.

After all, we weren't invited to the funeral. I wonder what would happen if the real story ever got out, if Mark played that video he still has.

No one's watched the video yet except Mark, who saw the beginning and stopped it. And I realize that it's the perfect way to say good-bye to Amy.

If we bury it, then we can say good-bye.

"I want to bury Amy," I whisper, to no one in particular.

Tristan catches my words, of course. He's too attentive sometimes, too interested in helping others for his own selfish reasons. A part of me loves him for it, but a larger part of me just wants to hit him until he realizes that this doesn't have to be his penance.

An even larger part of me knows it won't make a difference. Nothing will change the way he thinks.

"She's already buried."

"Thanks for that, Captain Obvious."

He pulls into the school parking lot and slides into a spot next to Cherry Bomb. Last week Mark decided he was going to start living life by screwing up everyone's expectations of him. He painted a frangipani on the side of his car like he's always wanted to do.

It's dumb, but a balloon of pride swelled up in my chest when he did it.

Tristan and I sit in the car, neither of us speaking. Our relationship is built around comfortable silences that neither of us feels a need to fill. After a while the right words come to me, so I say them. "I know she's already been buried, but I don't really think her spirit was in her body. We still have it, you know? It's in that dartboard, and it's in those crazy posters, and it's in that video Mark has."

Tristan nods, because he gets it. I love that he gets it. That he gets it—me—makes me kind of crazy about him.

"I'm ready to say good-bye," I tell him as his arms fold around me and he holds me so tight I think I'm going to break. "I want to say good-bye."

After school we head to the barn. Mark, Petal, Tristan, and I. We find the space on the floor that is the least covered in bird shit and push away the hay with our feet.

"Now what?" Petal asks.

"Now we get dirty," Mark says.

Like the nature boy he is, he drops to the ground and sinks his fingers into the earth. Damp and rich, it's easily moved beneath his fingers.

"Are you three going to help, or am I going to have to throw dirt at you?" He smiles sweetly up at us. Mark's words shoot straight these days. Always. The sideways words and sideways smiles floated away that day at the lake.

I drop to my knees, and Petal and Tristan follow. We all sink our fingers into the dirt. It goes on for a while, us digging through the sticky earth in the barn as if we're little kids playing in a sandpit.

Slide in fingers. Grab a bunch of soil. Flick it into growing pile.

Rinse. Repeat.

But there's no real rinsing; and by the time we're done, the dirt has wandered up my fingers and over my forearms. Black smudges cover us as we prepare to bury Amy.

"Deep enough?" Petal asks. "Wide enough?"

"It's grave-sized," I return. "A bit shallower, but I think that's okay."

I stand up, brush some of the dirt away by swiping it on my jeans. It clings to my shoes, my socks. When I walk, my feet smear dirt through the yellow hay.

Permanent stains.

Amy's death will be a permanent stain on my life. It's not going away. But goddammit, I'm going to learn to live with, and love, this stain. This will help me to . . . I don't know what. Be a better person? That's an untrue cliché. It will help me to find myself. This will—has already—drawn out elements of me that I didn't even know existed.

Apparently, I'm not half as bitchy as I thought.

"Ella?" Tristan shakes my shoulder. "You look a little spacey. Bad memories?" His lips tilt up at the edges.

Oh, right. We're standing in front of Amy's dartboard. Countless nights spent on her bed during the tenth grade when she first started smoking. I'd cough like anything to let her know I thought the habit was disgusting and then we'd throw darts at this board.

Good times.

The bad memories are more recent.

Pick Me Ups. Tristan, face full of fear and me yelling at him to just throw the fucking dart at me.

"Right," I say. "It's time to bury the memories."

Bad and good.

He helps me take down the dartboard and carry it over to the grave. Mark and Petal are standing by. Petal has the dress she borrowed from Amy the night of my seventeenth-birthday party and never got to give back. Mark has the records, wrapped up in crazy life-sized posters of Freddie Mercury and Cherie Currie.

He swallows, his Adam's apple bobbing up and down. "Should someone say something or something?"

"Or something," I say. I suck in a deep breath, smell the lovely bird shit stench that pervades the barn. There's something beautiful about how imperfect this is. "Let's watch the video."

Mark's brought his camera, and the memory card's in this time. We're all jostling for a glimpse of the tiny screen. I slide my fingers through Tristan's as Mark fiddles with his camera, trying to get the video to play.

Our hands fit perfectly and I draw comfort from his warmth, and Mark's and Petal's.

And then the video is on, and I get lost inside the fragmented images that roll across the screen.

Dark night. Silver stars.

Our bodies, heads cut off. The camera spins, topples onto the roof and then the world tilts on its axis. Blurry and terrifying and unknowable.

Our words are high-pitched knives in the dark, arrows zinging through the silence as we shred one another to pieces. Mark tells Amy that he saw her kissing me.

In the here and now, Petal looks surprised—maybe she was too out of it to remember that detail. Or maybe she had chosen to forget some memories of her own.

And then there's a cutoff image of Mark, his body only visible from the waist down. I watch the way his body language changes. Languid to fluid. Laid-back to intense. Rage, bitterness in the way his shoes bite into the tiles. His steps are so drawn into themselves that he barely makes a sound against the tiles of my rooftop. They don't flake and clatter away beneath his feet like they did under mine.

I can't see Amy or myself in any of the shots. But I can hear her laughing, laughing so wildly. And then I can hear the ceramic tiles falling away. That must have been when she spun around me like a ballerina, forcing me to dance with her and almost fall off the roof.

Her words, crackly but still so intense, come next. "I need Ella."

And then the jump.

Mark's bent down, his face swimming into the frame, yelling to Petal. Panic flickers, flames to life on his face. She stumbles into the frame and then she and Mark are both leaning down, and Petal's foot collides with the camera.

It tumbles farther down the roof, and suddenly Amy and I are on-screen. I'm slipping. Amy's already way over the edge, and I'm hanging on by just a few fingers.

Mark's fingers close around my wrist, and he's pulling and he's pulling and he's pulling. But right now, I'm not focused on him; I'm focused on the very edge of the camera screen. It's a shot of our hands, mine and Amy's, twined together.

At the very last second, when I'm yelling something incoherent and Mark's pulling so hard, Amy's fingers slip from mine.

I'm crying and crying and crying as I watch her fall off the screen.

Petal leans over the edge and makes a grab for her, but it's useless.

Then there are a series of brief, unfocused images and then darkness.

And in the barn, there is nothing but the sound of us breathing.

"She's gone," I say. "She's really gone."

And I'm weeping from the realization and the relief.

Because Amy, she pulled me right down to the brink of death with her, but I got a second chance at life. I got a second chance. And I wish, wish, wish that she'd gotten a second chance, too.

No one else seems to know what to say to that. There's silence for three heartbeats' time, then Mark breaks the memory card in half. Like Humpty Dumpty, like Amy, it can't be put back together again. He throws the halves into the grave. Tiny blue pieces of technology surrounded by huge walls of dirt.

It disappears into the hole we've dug, and Mark draws his sleeve across his eyes. I pat him on the back, and Petal puts her arms around his neck.

"It's better this way," she says. "It's better to remember and move on."

"Right," I say. "That's why we're here."

I lift the dartboard with both arms. "Good-bye," I whisper as I toss it into the grave.

My body still sometimes craves the adrenaline, the high-definition picture of the world that comes after the fall, after a dart zings past your head. But this is the end of it. Pick Me Ups won't be so hard to resist anymore. They're finally getting buried.

Petal flings the dress over the dartboard. "I've wanted to give this back to you for a while," she says as though Amy is there.

And who knows, maybe she is.

The records and posters, possibly the most important things in the world to Amy, go next. Then Mark reaches into his pocket and pulls out the purple scarf, the one that held all the photos.

"Nice breaking and entering, by the way," he says. "My next-door neighbor got an eyeful of your ass. He's a perv."

I wonder whether you should be allowed to mention things like that when you are saying farewell to your best friend.

"This was Amy's favorite scarf," Mark says. He unfolds it, revealing the photos from that night and dumping them into the grave.

We're all misty-eyed, but we don't acknowledge that we're crying. If no one speaks about it, we can always deny it later.

"We done?" Petal asks.

Tristan nods, as if to say *She was your friend; I don't have anything to add.*

Mark nods. He's done. Photos gone, posters gone, records breaking into the earth. Music for Amy's grave.

They all turn to me. I clear my throat. "I'm not done."

I pick up my backpack off the floor behind me and brush away the stray pieces of straw. I used to brush Amy's hair away from her face like that sometimes, when her bangs obscured her eyes.

Then I close my eyes and let myself feel the pain.

Because ignoring it isn't going to make it go away, no matter how hard I try.

I open my backpack and pull out the gnome. For the past month I've kept it in my bedroom, a constant link between Amy and myself. "I thought I should—" I stop speaking. There's no need. They know what I want to do, and they're in total agreement.

Good-bye, only witness to Amy's death.

Good-bye, Ref.

The gnome falls into the grave and smashes one of the records in half.

The shattered pieces sink into the damp earth, sticking out like wedges of pie.

"Now I'm done."

We all nod and get down on our knees again. We sweep the mound of dirt back into the grave. Bit by bit, we cover up the pieces of Amy's spirit. The spirit that deserved so much more. The pieces disappear, eventually, becoming a part of the earth.

The gnome is no longer watching.